BEST STORIES FROM THE

TEXAS
STORYTELLING
FESTIVAL

BEST STORIES FROM THE

TEXAS
STORYTELLING
FESTIVAL

COLLECTED AND EDITED BY
FINLEY STEWART

August House Publishers, Inc.
LITTLE ROCK

Permissions are included in the
section following the text.

Printed in the United States of America

10 9 8 7 6 5 4 3 2 1 HC
10 9 8 7 6 5 4 3 2 1 PB

LIBRARY OF CONGRESS CATALOGING-IN-PUBLICATION DATA

Best stories from the Texas Storytelling Festival /
edited by Finley Stewart.
p.   cm.
ISBN 0-87483-404-X (HB : alk. paper) : $25.00 —
ISBN 0-87483-405-8 (PB : alk. paper) : $15.00
1. Tales. 2. Tales—Texas. I. Stewart, Finley, 1962–
II. Texas Storytelling Festival.
GR76.B47   1995
398.2'09764—dc20   94-48478

Executive editor: Liz Parkhurst
Assistant editors: Debbie Tarvin, Seale Pylate, Sue T. Williams
Design director: Ted Parkhurst
Cover design: Harvill Ross Studios Ltd.

For my mother, Little Bit,
the true storyteller of my family,
in her seventy-second year

Acknowledgments

There's a long list of people who have helped make this publication a reality, and to each of them I owe a great deal of thanks. For the last three years Liz and Ted Parkhurst have kept me in check—quietly reminding me that this book needed to be done, and that they were willing to do it. For the last year, Liz has constantly reworked schedules and deadlines, overlooked my procrastination, and understood emerging barriers. Many thanks go to Liz, Ted, Debbie, Seale, and all of the August House staff.

Since this book is really the product of ten years of festivals, it is important to recognize those people who have helped the festival emerge as a national jewel: thanks to Nancy Craig Scott, Dr. Jim Thomas, Letty Watt, Jeannine Beekman, Jim Ohmart, Mary Ann Brewer, Paul Porter, Gene Richardson, Karen Morgan, and Joan Terrell, past and present members of the TSA Board of Directors, including Barbara McBride-Smith, Zinita Fowler, J.B. Keith, Tom McDermott, Harriet Lewis, Sally Goodroe, Rob Schneider Jr., James Ford, Sharon Moa, Elaine Hampshire, and Rosanna Herndon; with a special thanks to Herbert Holl and the Greater Denton Arts Council.

We all owe a great debt to Liz Faulk and John Henry Faulk—to Liz for her permission and blessing on our use of John Henry's stories, and to John Henry for leaving the world a better place because of them.

My sincerest appreciation goes to Jimmy Neil Smith and Susan O'Connor for years of help, encouragement, and friendship.

Most of my computer typesetting was painstakingly done by my best friend in the whole wide world—Sylvia Pitchford. I thank her for years of help and counsel, and for putting up with the hundreds of strange storytellers who help make up my world.

—F.S.

Contents

Introduction

Everyone has a storyteller in his or her family—a person known to be the keeper of the family tales. For me, it was—and is—my mother. She didn't tell Cinderella or The Three Little Pigs, nor did she read fairy tales to me each night. What she *did* was tell stories—to everyone, and I mean everyone—about our family. Of my weird Uncle Bill. Of my grandfather bringing her and her family to Dallas in a covered wagon in the mid-1920s. Of the day Daddy went to church.

You have a storyteller in your family, too. It may be your father, mother, grandmother, husband, wife, son, or daughter. If you can't immediately think who it could be, then chances are it's you! Yes, you! You see, we all tell stories—every day. In fact, in our own environment, when we feel safe and comfortable, we all tell stories well. Really well. Some say we must tell stories. So much so that some textbooks from modern anthropologists now describe mankind not as *homo sapiens* but as *homo narrans*, that is, man as narrator. In a very real sense, we tell stories to remind us and others of who we are. Our stories pass on values, beliefs, and histories; they legislate cultures and mores. Even scientists have determined that what makes us unique as a species is our ability to communicate our stories.

Clearly, the modern world is catching up with one of our oldest known folkways: storytelling. While we all tell stories, there are a growing number of people who have elevated the common folkway into a recognizable art form. Taking to the road with their storytelling wares, they tell stories as a practice of art—modern pied pipers of an all but forgotten art form.

Contained in this anthology are some of the best stories from some of the best storytellers of our time. Each year these tellers gather at our annual Texas Storytelling Festival to share and tell tales and encourage others to do the same. Founded just a decade ago, the festival has grown to be one of the premier storytelling events in the nation, a place where everyone's ability to listen and tell is affirmed and nurtured.

In 1986, Dr. Ted Colson, James Howard, and Sylvia Pitchford helped make the festival a reality, and many of the accolades and thanks must go to those three key people who helped make that first event possible. That first March, when both listeners and tellers came to Denton, little was known about storytelling across the state or in our region. A small festival existed in Oklahoma City, and there were rumors of "a woman who told stories" who lived in Dallas.

That woman was Elizabeth Ellis. When we first began calling folks to participate, Elizabeth gladly agreed. She was joined that year by other regional tellers: Rosanna Herndon, Ted Colson, Zinita Fowler, and the StoryWeavers (James Howard and Finley Stewart).

We had envisioned it as a statewide festival, but it gathered tellers from across the Southwest. People who called themselves storytellers came from Oklahoma, Louisiana, and Texas. The Folktellers—Barbara Freeman and Connie Regan-Blake of North Carolina—even agreed to join us. It was a surprise to all of us that there were so many people who valued the art and practice of the well-told tale—and even a bigger surprise that until that festival, none of us knew each other.

By the end of the festival a woman by the name of Jeannine Beekman from a place called Houston had agreed to help for the next year. So did two other women by the names of Barbara McBride-Smith and Letty Watt, both living in someplace called Oklahoma. All in all, there were eighty-four people that first year, and we were astounded that that many people had come to hear and tell stories. By 1994, festival attendance had swelled to over 2,500—coming from nineteen different states.

Between now and then, an organization was founded. Today the Tejas Storytelling Association unites lovers of stories from throughout Texas and the great Southwest on both regional and local levels. Already, TSA has gained more than 600 members from fourteen states. The organization strives to preserve the traditional art of storytelling, while at the same time opening avenues of exploration to place storytelling once again in the heart of our modern civilization.

Through the years, the Texas Storytelling Festival has featured such notable tellers as Jackie Torrence, Jay O'Callahan, Heather Forest, Carol Birch, and Laura Simms—just to name a few. But without question, the festival's strongest reputation has been that of bringing new voices to the forefront of the storytelling movement. The festival has helped firmly establish the careers of tellers like Barbara McBride-Smith, Charlotte Byrn, Jeannine Beekman, Jay Stailey, and many more. It has also celebrated longtime Texas raconteurs like Elizabeth Ellis, Gayle Ross, and John Henry Faulk. In special segments of the festival, the new rising talent of our region has been showcased, and included here from amongst them are the works of Mary Ann Brewer, Nancy Burks, James Ford, Harriet Lewis, and Fran Stallings. Here, as nowhere else, regional and local tellers gather to support and nurture each other. It's those voices this collection aims to celebrate and pay homage to.

Each spring, the festival continues. As the bluebonnets begin their bloom, the voices of the very best tellers in the nation can be heard drifting

Mr. Cramer:
A True Ghost Story of Houston

JEANNINE PASINI BEEKMAN

My mother, Lucille Hanks Pasini, was a fabulous ghost-story teller. I was a child when she first told me about Mr. Cramer. It has been my good fortune to visit with people who have heard Mr. Cramer, and everything I have included in my version is true. Although I've never heard him, I still trust that my chance will come, and I only hope Mr. Cramer isn't avoiding me for disseminating this story so widely.

Mr. Cramer was the caretaker of the library. He was just as much a part of it as the books and the shelves and the tables. So when the beautiful Spanish Renaissance building opened in 1926, he just naturally moved into it with the rest of the fixtures. Mr. Cramer had no home but the library. He lived in a small room in the basement. But he did not live there alone. He shared his life with his two most precious companions: his violin and his shepherd dog, Pete.

Every night, after the library was locked up tight, Mr. Cramer went down to his basement room and picked up his fiddle. Then he and Pete climbed up the narrow concrete steps to the ground floor. They walked along the red tiled floor to the main staircase. Then they climbed up, up, up to the very top of the library. He perched on the balcony railing, and there, under the high carved rotunda ceiling, late into the night, Mr. Cramer played the beautiful "Blue Danube Waltz" for all of his friends. He played for Shakespeare and Socrates; he played for Chekhov and Churchill; he played for Plutarch, Puccini, and Pete.

Mr. Cramer loved the library. He took great pride in keeping it just so. He mopped and waxed the red tiled floors until they shone like glass. He buffed the oak furniture with beeswax, lemon oil, and plenty of elbow grease until it gleamed. Nose prints and finger smudges were soon dispatched with hot soapy water and ammonia, and the windows were polished up with newspaper until they sparkled like diamonds when the sun shines. But his special care was saved for the books. He had a secret mixture that he rubbed into the old leather bindings to keep them supple and smooth.

In summer, when the loggia windows were opened wide to catch whatever Gulf breeze there was, the dust and grit that came in too never had a chance to settle between the pages. Mr. Cramer was always there. He'd pull a clean rag from the back pocket of his bib overalls and brush every speck away. Sometimes he wondered what it would be like to take down any book he pleased, carry it out to the loggia, sit in one of the wicker chairs under the ceiling fan for as long as he chose, and just read. He couldn't. But whenever he had a hankering for a book, he only had to walk a mile down the road to the Colored Carnegie Library and borrow any book he wanted. It bothered him that the bindings were ragged and some of the pages were torn. But he soon came to know them all as friends as well.

Mr. Cramer loved living things. When an old bur oak on the east side of the library entrance died, a sapling sprang from the roots, and he knew the old tree would come back on its own. He took an acorn, planted it in a pot, and tended it in his basement room. When the seedling had grown strong enough to stand on its own, he planted it on the west side of the entrance. He must have done a good job because there it stands to this day. It provides a nice bit of shade and quiet amidst the noise and diesel fumes of the city.

Then, in 1936, his quiet life reached its end. The librarians came to work and found the building locked up tight. They made their way down the narrow concrete steps to the basement and found Mr. Cramer cold and still in his narrow bed. He had died in his sleep and left as gently as he lived. He had no people as far as anyone knew, so the librarians took up a collection to have him buried. The mortuary men laid him out real nice.

They dressed him in a clean pair of bib overalls, put him in a plain pine box, and placed his fiddle in his hands. They carried him to the cemetery in Freedmen's Town. It would have been nice if he could have been buried in Founder's Cemetery with the poets and the politicians. He couldn't. But this was a pretty place too, with a nice piece of shade, just the sort of spot Mr. Cramer loved. The preacher spoke a few words over the coffin, and a librarian remembered him as having the sweetest smile of anyone she had ever seen. Then they lowered him into the red clay earth.

But as they began to shovel in the dirt, someone saw a dog among the tombstones. It was a shepherd dog that looked an awful lot like Pete. They called and whistled. But the dog ran away. If it was Pete, all they could do was hope someone found him and gave him a good home.

Now it wasn't too long after that when strange things began to happen in the library. The children noticed it first. They complained that someone was playing music, and it kept them from getting their homework done. Their mothers thought this was a novel excuse, but the librarians were more sympathetic. They said that it was just the sound of the wind blowing through Mr. Cramer's oak tree; the tree had a music all its own. Then others heard it. No-nonsense businessmen would raise their eyes from their perusal of the *Wall Street Journal* and cock their heads as if listening to the strains of a distant waltz. Then the mothers and even the librarians heard it. It started in the basement and floated up the narrow concrete steps to the ground floor. It drifted above the red tiled floor to the main staircase, and then it rose up, up, up to the very top of the library. There, under the high carved rotunda ceiling, it reached a crescendo and faded away.

When the modern granite and glass library opened in 1976, people wondered if Mr. Cramer would cease his solitary wanderings. But there are people who will tell you that they have been in the beautiful old Spanish Renaissance building and heard footsteps on the main staircase. When they turned to look, there was no one there. They will say that they have heard something that sounds like the beautiful "Blue Danube Waltz" reach a crescendo under the high carved rotunda ceiling and then fade away. And they will swear to you that they have heard the unmistakable *click, click, click, click* of a dog's nails walking upon a red tiled floor.

MARY ANN BREWER is a native Oklahoman from an old Texas family. As a young woman, she studied Spanish in Mexico at El Instituto Tecnologico y de Estudios Superiores de Monterrey, and she fell in love with the Spanish language and the Latin culture. She teaches Spanish to young children and uses storytelling as a primary teaching tool. She is a sought-after presenter at teacher workshops and institutes. Mary Ann lives in Richardson, Texas, and is currently at work on a major textbook project.

La Cucarachita

MARY ANN BREWER

Although the story of the lovely little cockroach and her spouse the mouse has its roots in Spain, many Latin American countries claim it as their own. I once witnessed three teachers—a Cuban, a Puerto Rican, and a Mexican—arguing at length about Cucarachita's country of origin. They never reached a consensus, but they did agree about one thing: they all loved the story. So do I.

Once there was a little cockroach, and her name was Cucarachita. One day while she was cleaning her house, she found a golden coin, *encontró una moneda de oro.*

"*Ya soy linda y también rica,* now I have good looks and money, too!" she said. "The only thing I need now is a husband, *me falta esposo."*

So she went looking for one. The first likely candidate she found was Señor Perro, the dog.

"*Buenos días, Señor Perro,"* said Cucarachita, batting her big cockroach eyes at the prospective husband.

"*Buenos días, Cucarachita."* Señor Perro stopped. He was always glad to see Cucarachita.

"*Señor Perro, ¿quieres casarte con una cucarachita que es linda y también rica?* Would you like to marry a cute little cockroach with good looks and money too?" she said, showing him the golden coin.

Señor Perro had never really considered the possibility of marrying Cucarachita. After all, she was an insect. But the golden coin got his attention. He thought a moment and replied, "*Sí, Cucarachita. Quiero casarme contigo,* I want to marry you."

"*Bueno, Señor Perro, ¿cómo me cantarás si me caso contigo?* How will you sing to me if I marry you?"

"*Cucarachita, yo te cantaré así,* I will sing to you like this." Then Señor Perro stood up very straight, raised his nose up very high, and let loose with a terrible loud howl. "*Aaaa-ooooooooooooo!"*

Cucarachita made a face and clapped her delicate pinchers over her cute little cockroach ears. "*Señor Perro, lo siento, pero no me gusta esta canción.* I'm sorry, but I don't like the song. *No puedo casarme contigo,* I can't marry you."

Señor Perro shrugged his shoulders, waved goodbye, and continued to walk on down the street. Cucarachita kept looking for a husband. It wasn't long before the second likely candidate appeared on the street. It was Señor Gato, the cat.

"*Buenos días, Señor Gato,*" Cucarachita said, batting those beautiful cockroach eyes in the cat's direction.

"*Buenos días, Cucarachita,*" the cat replied, with only a glance in Cucarachita's direction.

Señor Gato started to hurry on his way, but Cucarachita stopped him. "*Señor Gato, ¿quieres casarte con una cucarachita que es linda y también rica?* Would you like to marry a cute little cockroach with good looks and money too?" she said, showing him the golden coin.

Señor Gato took one look at that golden coin, and he became very interested in this idea. "*¡Sí, sí, sí, Cucarachita! Quiero casarme contigo,* I want to marry you."

"*Bueno, Señor Gato, ¿cómo me cantarás si me caso contigo?* How will you sing to me if I marry you?"

"*Cucarachita, yo te cantaré así,* I will sing to you like this." Señor Gato cleared his throat, threw back his head, and screeched an ear-piercing *"Mmmeeeoooowww!"*

Cucarachita bent down her head and tried to cover it with all six of her cute little cockroach feet. When the commotion was over, she looked up cautiously. "*Señor Gato, me asustarías por la noche,* you would scare me at night. *No puedo casarme contigo,* I can't marry you," she said.

Señor Gato hung his head in disappointment and slowly walked down the street. Cucarachita kept looking for a husband. Then she saw him! The cutest little mouse in the neighborhood, Ratoncito Pérez.

"*Buenos días, Ratoncito Pérez,*" Cucarachita said, once more batting those beautiful cockroach eyes.

"*Buenos días, Cucarachita,*" squeaked Ratoncito Pérez, smiling shyly.

"*Ratoncito Pérez, ¿quieres casarte con una cucarachita que es linda y también rica?* Would you like to marry a cute little cockroach with good looks and money too?" she said, showing him that golden coin.

Ratoncito Pérez raised his eyebrows in surprise. He had always thought Cucarachita to be the cutest cockroach in town. "*Sí, Cucarachita. Yo quiero casarme contigo.*"

"*Bueno, Ratoncito Pérez, ¿cómo me cantarás si me caso contigo?*"

"*Cucarachita, yo te cantaré así,* I will sing to you like this..." Ratoncito Pérez began to squeak out a lovely little rendition of the famous Mexican folksong "La Cucaracha."

Cucarachita could hardly believe her cute little cockroach ears. "*Ay, Ratoncito Pérez. ¡Qué canción tan bonita!* What a pretty song! Yes, I'll marry you. *¡Sí, yo me casaré contigo!*"

Cucarachita did not believe in long engagements. They planned the wedding for the next day. She got up very early in the morning to put a big pot of beans on the stove to cook, *una olla grande de frijoles con tocino*. The beans were seasoned with lots of bacon. They would be for the party, *la fiesta de la boda*, that would follow the wedding.

The sun was not too high in the sky when Ratoncito Pérez arrived at Cucarachita's house. He knocked at the door, and when she opened it, Ratoncito Pérez nearly went into a swoon. Surprisingly, it was not from the sight of Cucarachita's beautiful little face, but from the wonderful smell of the bacon in those beans. There is not a mouse in this world who can resist a big juicy piece of bacon, and Ratoncito Pérez was no exception.

"*Cucarachita, dáme un pedacito de tocino, por favor, mi amor*, just a little piece of bacon, please, my love."

"*¡Ay, no Ratoncito Pérez! Es para la fiesta*, it's for the party. Now come with me. It's time to leave for the church, *vámonos para la iglesia.*"

Down the street the little couple strolled, claw in claw, *tomados de las.* Cucarachita was a beaming bride, *era una novia radiante.* But Ratoncito Pérez's mind was somewhere else. He could not get the thought of that bacon out of his mind, *continuó pensando en el tocino.*

"*Me gusta el tocino*, I *do* like bacon," he thought, his mouth watering. "*Me encanta el tocino*, that bacon has me in a spell." He became slightly wild-eyed. "*¡Tengo que comer el tocino!* I've got to have that bacon!" Ratoncito Pérez was consumed with only one thought—the bacon!

At the door of the church, a trembling Ratoncito Pérez turned to Cucarachita. "*Cucarachita, me olvidé mis guantes*, I've forgotten my gloves. They're at your house. Wait for me here at the church, *espérame en la iglesia. Yo volveré en seguida*, I'll be right back!"

Before Cucarachita had time to answer, Ratoncito Pérez turned and ran back toward her house, leaving a bewildered Cucarachita at the altar—*una novia sin novio*, a bride without her groom.

Ratoncito Pérez opened the front door of the house and hurried into the kitchen. He climbed up onto the stove, *se subió a la estufa*, then onto the big pot of beans with bacon, *la olla grande de frijoles con tocino.* There, out in the center of the pot, was a nice, big, juicy piece of bacon bubbling and bubbling, *un pedazo sabroso de tocino.* Ratoncito Pérez balanced himself on the edge of that big pot and oh-so-carefully stretched one claw out over the boiling hot beans—trying to get … that … bacon … *tratando de cojer … el … tocino …*

Meanwhile, Cucarachita was waiting and pacing and crying and sighing. "*¿Ratoncito Pérez? ¿Dónde está mi Ratoncito Pérez?*" Then she became tired and angry. "I'm tired of this, *estoy cansada. Me voy a mi casa*, I'm going home!" And Cucarchita walked out of the church and started down the street toward home.

When she entered her house it was dark, *la casa estaba oscura.* She was tired, but she was also a little bit hungry. "I'm just going to have some beans and go to bed, *voy a comer unos frijoles y acostarme.*"

She walked into the kitchen; she turned on the light; she picked up a bowl and a spoon; and she slowly walked over to the stove. Then Cucarachita looked down into the big pot of beans, *miró en la olla grande ...*

"*¡RATONCITO PEREZ, mi amor!*"

Pobrecito Ratoncito Pérez, estaba flotando entre los frijoles. The poor little mouse was floating face down in the beans!

Pobrecita Cucarachita, poor little Cucarachita. She spent the rest of her days crying and sighing, *llorando y suspirando por Ratoncito Pérez.*

And nobody ever got to marry that cute little cockroach with good looks and money too ... *la cucarachita que era linda y también rica.*

Tío Conejo and the Hurricane

MARY ANN BREWER

He came from Africa, the beloved trickster of a rich and varied culture. He was embraced in the Americas and given several names—Br'er Rabbit in the American South, Hermano Conejo (Brother Rabbit) in Mexico, and Tío Conejo (Uncle Rabbit) in parts of Central and South America. Although Tío Conejo has many opponents, in this story we meet my favorite—Señor Tigre.

A long time ago, all the animals in the jungle got along with each other, except for one, Tiger, better known as Señor Tigre. Señor Tigre vowed to eat all the small animals he could get his claws on, and he loved to chase after Rabbit, better known as Tío Conejo.

Pero Tío Conejo era listo y vivo, but Tío Conejo was quick and smart, and he loved to play tricks on slow, gullible Señor Tigre. Like the time when Tío Conejo was cleaning out some vines and making a rope out of them, *estaba haciendo una cuerda.* It was hot, *hacía mucho calor,* and the sun was blazing down. Tío Conejo wasn't paying any attention, when who should come sneaking up behind him? Why, his favorite enemy, *su enemigo favorito—el gato malo y tonto,* that mean dumb cat, Señor Tigre.

"OK, Tío Conejo, *ya te pesqué,* I've caught you now. *Tu eres un conejo muerto*—you are one dead rabbit!"

Señor Tigre was too close. Tío Conejo knew he didn't have time to get away. He had to think fast. "OK, Señor Tigre, *cómeme, cómeme ahorita.* Just eat me up right now. *No quiero quedarme aquí cuando—suceda.* I don't want to be around when—it happens!" Tío Conejo gave a little shiver of fear and rolled his eyes dramatically.

"*¿Suceda? ¿Suceda qué?* What's going to happen, Tío Conejo?"

"Oh, Señor Tigre, haven't you heard? *El huracán viene,* a terrible hurricane's coming. It'll be here any minute. This sudden heat is a sure sign, *este calor es un signo seguro.*"

"*¿El huracán? ¡A mi no me gustan los huracanes!*" Señor Tigre replied with a shaky voice.

"I know you don't like hurricanes. I don't like them either. That's why I'm making this rope. I'm going to tie myself down to something so I don't

23

blow away. *No quiero volarme con el aire.*" Tío Conejo held up his rope for Señor Tigre's inspection.

"That's a good idea, Tío Conejo. *Pero espérate un momentito,* but you just wait a minute! I want you to tie *me* down. *No quiero volarme con el aire tampoco,* I don't want to blow away either."

"Oh, Señor Tigre, I like the way your mind works. Let's see what we can find to tie you down to." Tío Conejo's eyes danced as he grabbed Señor Tigre by the paw and led him through the jungle. Suddenly, Tío Conejo stopped short. "Oh, Señor Tigre, look at this big tamarind tree, *este árbol de tamarindo.* I bet it has stood right here through lots of hurricanes. Let's tie you to this!"

"OK, *pero, bien fuerte.*"

"Oh yeah … good and tight, I'll tie you good and tight!" Tío Conejo couldn't help but smile.

So Tío Conejo tied Señor Tigre to that tamarind tree with his long rope of vines, wrapping it around and around Señor Tigre's chest. "*¿Bien fuerte,* Señor Tigre? Tight enough?"

But Señor Tigre was still uncertain. "*Un poquito más fuerte,* just a little tighter, Tío Conejo."

So Tío Conejo grabbed the rope with both paws and pulled with all his might. "*¿Bien fuerte ya?* Tight enough now?"

Señor Tigre's eyes nearly bulged out of his head. He managed to gasp out, "*¡Bien fuerte!*" But when he looked at the other end of the rope, Tío Conejo was nowhere to be found. *Tío Conejo se fué como una chispa*—Tío Conejo was outta there!

Now it should come as no surprise that Señor Tigre was not the most popular guy in the jungle, *no era muy popular.* It took him well into the next day just to find someone who was willing to untie him. *No se liberó hasta el día siguiente.* He finally talked a couple of monkeys into letting him loose. Just as they untied him, he grabbed one of the monkeys and started to pop it into his mouth, *estaba por comerse el mono.* At that moment he heard a voice up in the tree. *Oyó una voz allá en el árbol.*

"Uh-uh-uh! That's no way to eat a monkey, Señor Tigre. Don't you know how to eat a monkey? *¿No sabes cómo se come un mono?*"

"Well, I *thought* I knew how to eat a monkey. *Pues, creí que sabía.*"

"No, Señor Tigre. You've got to throw that monkey up into the air, close your eyes, open your mouth, and let the monkey fall in. That's how you eat a monkey!"

Señor Tigre scratched his head slowly and repeated the instructions. "*'¿Tira el mono, cierra los ojos, abre la boca, y déjalo caer en la boca?' Así lo haré,* OK. I'll do it like that. Here goes!"

Señor Tigre closed his eyes, opened his mouth, threw that monkey up in the air—and waited. But the monkey caught a branch of the tree, and he was gone, *el mono huyó.*

Tío Conejo was waiting in that tree, *estaba esperando en el árbol.* He had a big tamarind seed, and as soon as he got a good aim, he threw that big old seed right down Señor Tigre's throat, *la tiró en la garganta del Señor Tigre.* Oh, Señor Tigre was in terrible shape. He was coughing and sputtering, trying to get his breath. Finally, he blew that tamarind seed through the air, *la sopló por el aire.* Then he ran back into the jungle, yelling for Tío Conejo, *corrió por la selva, gritando el nombre del Tío Conejo.*

Now, some people say that he's still out there—that somewhere in the thick, green, Latin American jungle lurks a slow, dull-witted, big cat with a bad temper. They say you can hear him as he runs through the jungle, yelling for Tío Conejo. "Tío Conejo, *algún día te pescaré,* someday I'm going to catch you! *Tu eres un conejo muerto,* you are one dead rabbit!"

But you'll never hear Tío Conejo answer back. He's nowhere to be found. *Tío Conejo se fué como una chispa*—Tío Conejo is outta there!

JIM BURKS

NANCY BURKS is a full-time professional storyteller, an accomplished musician, ventriloquist, and actress, having performed roles as diverse as Titania in Shakespeare's *A Midsummer Night's Dream* and Medea in Euripides' tale. She and her crocodile pal Larry travel Texas, carrying fun and the joy of storytelling to schoolchildren. She has recently published a book of scripts for ventriloquists. Nancy performed "Maid Maleen," her own version of a Grimm Brothers story, at the Texas Festival in 1994. She lives in Granbury with her husband, Jim, and her children, Brody and Emily.

Maid Maleen

NANCY BURKS

I tell lots of different kinds of stories, but fairy tales are still my first love. I try to remain true to the spirit of the story, but I am not above editing to further a particular value or make a point. After all, isn't that what storytellers have always done? "Maid Maleen" appears in several versions, most notably in the tales of the Brothers Grimm. I believe that she is a modern woman caught in more restrictive times. Yet she has an adventure, overcomes a rather large obstacle, and still finds time for romance. What a woman! When I told "Maid Maleen" at the Texas Festival, the final confrontation takes place in Princess Esme's sleeping chambers. I have here presented a less "torrid" version in order to reach a wider audience, but as you read, let your imagination be your guide.

Once there was a young woman, the daughter of a king, whose name was Maid Maleen. She was beautiful and delicate, her needlework was beyond reproach, and she could sing like a bird. Of these things her father was very proud.

She was also intelligent and resourceful, creative and courageous, and exceedingly strong-willed. Of these things her father was not so proud, thinking them unseemly in a young woman.

Maleen had met and fallen in love with a young man named Roland, who was the son of a neighboring king. He admired Maleen's flawless skin and the curtain of honey-colored hair that fell down her back. He also admired her intelligence, courage, and determination. Maleen's father disapproved and ordered her to send Roland away. She refused. "Our love," she said, "is a rare and precious thing."

The king became very upset and chose to deal with Maleen's disobedience strongly. He ordered built a round, stone tower, as tall as the castle's highest parapet. No windows were built into the design. Into the castle he place food and water enough for seven years ... and Maid Maleen.

As the lone workman mortared in the final brick, he heard Maleen whisper, "... a rare and precious love."

Every day of the first year of her imprisonment, Roland could be seen pacing around the stone tower on his handsome stallion, calling out

27

Maleen's name. From within, Maleen called out Roland's name, but neither could hear the other.

On the first day of the second year of her imprisonment, war broke out between the two kingdoms, and Roland was called away to lead his father's armies. Believing that Maleen had surely perished within, he agreed.

On the first day of the third year of her captivity, Maleen's yearning for the sun eclipsed even her yearning for the sight of Roland, and she began with a butter knife to chip away at the mortar in the wall.

On the first day of the fourth year of her captivity, Maleen's patient knife broke through to the sun, and she kissed the sunbeam where it lay upon the stone floor.

On the first day of the fifth year of her captivity, Maleen's window on the world was large enough that she could see in the distance the castle where she had spent her childhood.

On the first day of the sixth year of her captivity, the window showed her the castle, the surrounding fields, and the village as they lay in ruins, barren and deserted. Maid Maleen realized that she would have to be her own hero.

On the first day of the seventh year of her captivity, Maid Maleen pushed through the window, dropped to the ground, and went off in search of her rare and precious love.

She found Roland's castle still standing, and presented herself at the kitchen door. She was immediately given a job in the scullery.

Through the kitchen gossip, Maleen found out that Roland did indeed still live, and that he was scheduled to be married in seven days. The princess had been chosen by the king. Roland apparently showed no interest in the choosing of the bride; indeed, he had not yet even seen her. The Princess Esme was said to be hiding herself in her chambers. Roland's heart, they said, lay dead and buried with a girl in a tall stone tower.

Maid Maleen decided that even if he were lost to her, she had to see Roland again, and to meet his bride. She asked for and received the job of lady-in-waiting to the Princess Esme.

What a horrible woman! Maid Maleen had never met a colder heart. She had never experienced a more bitter disposition! She had never seen an uglier face! Now in all fairness, it wasn't the features themselves, but the look of complete disapproval and snobbery that made the girl so unfortunately unattractive. Maleen realized easily enough why Princess Esme hid herself form Roland. No matter how brokenhearted he was, he surely would have realized that he did not want to marry this woman!

On the wedding day, Maid Maleen was called before the princess. "I have hurt my ankle," said Esme, "and I cannot walk today. You must walk the bridal path before me and stand in the church to say the vows. Then when it's all over, I will be waiting for Roland in my chambers. I hate all that walking, and I hate having those awful unwashed crowds of commoners looking at me. You do it!"

Joy and horror fought for supremacy in Maleen's heart. She was overjoyed at the thought of seeing Roland again, but to marry him only to have him turned over to another … Maid Maleen however, was not the sort of woman to stand idly by and watch the strands of fate unwind themselves. She agreed.

Maleen was dressed in a beautiful gown of royal purple, and a heavy veil was placed over her face. She walked out into the garden to meet Roland.

He was exactly as Maleen remembered him … except that the joy and love she remembered upon his face were replaced by a look of sadness and loss. They began their walk to the church.

They had not gone far before they came to a place where the nettles had overgrown the road. A childhood song sprang to Maid Maleen's mind and she sang out:

> Nettles, nettles, move aside,
> make way for the true bride!

Roland looked for the first time at the girl by his side. Something in her voice untied one of the strands of grief that held captive his heart. Could it be …?

They walked on in silence, consumed by their own thoughts, until they came to a spot in the road where the doves gathered to pick gravel. The second verse of the song burst from Maid Maleen's lips:

> Dove, dove, fly aside,
> make way for the true bride!

Again Roland jumped with surprise, and looked for the first time closely at the girl. Beneath her heavy veil hung her long, long hair, just the color of dark honey in the sun. Just the color of … could it be …?

The two walked in silence until they came to the church, whose doors were closed against the wind. Maleen sang out the third verse of the song:

> Church doors, church doors, open wide,
> make way for the true bride!

Roland reached to take his bride's hand, and when their flesh touched, they both knew.

The church doors opened, the vows were said, and Roland and Maleen were whisked away to their separate chambers. She was relieved of her beautiful purple gown, given back her gray serving smock, and pushed unceremoniously out the door.

In her chambers, Princess Esme was waiting, dressed in a flowing gown of red. She sat at the dining table, which was adorned by candles trimmed to their lowest point. Unfortunately for Esme, not even full darkness would have fooled Roland. He knew that this was not the girl he had married in the church that day.

Roland took the chair across from Esme and smiled at her. The candle-light flickered across his handsome face, and darkness pooled in the dimples there.

"Darling, tell me … what was it that you sang to the nettles today?"

Princess Esme sighed at Roland's look, but she would not be fooled by silly questions asked by a prince. She had been warned that a princess was often tested on her wedding night. "Nettles!" she said. "I don't sing to nettles! Do you think I am a fool?"

Actually, Roland did indeed think that Princess Esme was at least a little bit of a fool, but he didn't say so. Instead he leaned across the candle and took Esme's smooth pink hand in his own rough dark one. He turned it over and kissed her palm.

"My dear," he said, "tell me, what was it that you sang to the dove today?"

Princess Esme was, of course, quite uninterested in doves, and she was extremely tired of the whole conversation. Knowing that a prince would want a no-nonsense answer, she laughed and said, "Dove? I don't sing to doves! Do I look to you like a ninny?"

Actually, Roland did indeed think that the princess looked at least a little like a ninny, but he didn't say so. Instead, he leaned over the table and stroked Esme's hair.

"Dearest," he said, "tell me … what was it that you sang today to the church doors?"

Now Esme knew that the prince was simply playing some stupid game, and she was quite ready for it to be finished. With more than a touch of irritation in her voice she replied:

"Church doors! I don't sing to church doors! Do I look to you like an idiot?"

Actually, that's exactly what she looked like to Roland, but he didn't say so. Instead he rose from his chair and went around to hold Esme's chair for her. Thinking that he wanted to dance, Esme rose with a smile on her face. She held out her hands and Roland took them. Spinning her around, he planted his booted foot firmly in her rather ample backside and gave her a kick that propelled her toward the door. In a rousing baritone voice he sang to her:

Woman, woman, stand aside,
make way for the true bride!

Princess Esme burst into tears and ran from the room, on her way out passing Maid Maleen, who was on her way in. Maleen threw herself into Roland's arms and covered his face with kisses. They were married and lived for many, many happy years, producing a great number of children and grandchildren. Which, of course, only goes to prove that a rare and precious love will always find its way.

HAPPY BYRN DUMAS

CHARLOTTE PUGH BYRN, a retired first-grade teacher and elementary school librarian, was born and reared in the small town of Hamburg, Ashley County, Arkansas, in the southeast corner of the state. Had not World War II come along, she would have probably lived out her life never more than a stone's throw from the house in which she was reared. But World War II did come along, and the world and Charlotte will never be the same. Charlotte's stories are a blending of her simple, small-town beginning and a more exotic life as she accompanied her career Air Force husband all over the world. She was a featured teller at the 1994 National Storytelling Festival, but told first on the Texas Storytelling Festival stage.

Speculation

CHARLOTTE PUGH BYRN

Stock? What's that? The only kind of stock I knew anything about was live *stock—until, that is, my husband introduced me to the stock market in the summer of 1955. I'm still not an investor—but I do know how to read the stock market report in the daily paper. Well, at least that's something, isn't it?*

I am not a gambler. Well, best I clarify that statement—I would be an avid gambler if I could be assured that every time I gambled I would win—so I guess it is not so much that I am not a gambler as it is that I am a poor loser—a very poor loser. So I don't gamble.

Now my husband, Dub, was not exactly a gambler, but he did enjoy the stock market. Not that we ever had much money for him to invest in stock, but he would diligently chart several stocks that he thought showed promise. He would rush out and get the morning paper each day, look up "his" stocks and chart their progress on graph paper. If one of "his" stocks had gone up—well, you would have thought he was a major stockholder in the company, he would be so happy. If, however, "his" stock had gone down in value, his whole day would be ruined. Occasionally he would buy a very few shares of some stock that he thought had potential. So on July 22, 1990, when I received a letter from Pepsi Cola Company announcing a stock split, it put me to reminiscing. My thoughts traveled all the way back to June of 1955 ...

Dub was a career pilot in the Air Force. We were stationed in Tacoma, Washington, when orders came for the entire group to be transferred to Moses Lake, just east of the mountains. Now usually Air Force families looked forward to transfers that involved the whole group, because that meant that all of your friends would be going, too. So would your enemies, true, but you could continue to ignore them. However, for this transfer we had a big problem. Our problem was a teenaged daughter who was very much into Girl Scouting—and she wanted to go to Girl Scout summer camp with her Tacoma troop. That troop camped up at Coeur d'Alene, Idaho, on the lake. It was a beautiful campsite—so I couldn't blame her for wanting to go there to camp. Still, we *had* to move.

Finally, her father said, "Happy, we have to move—but I'll make this agreement with you. You go on and register for summer camp with your Tacoma troop, and when the time comes for camp we'll bring you back to Tacoma and you can go on the camp bus up to camp. Then, two weeks later, we will come back and meet the bus and take you back to Moses Lake." So the matter was settled and we made the move.

True to his word, when camp time came, we took Happy back to Tacoma and put her on the bus for camp. All was well.

A few days before it was time to go back to Tacoma and meet the bus, Dub came in from work one afternoon and said, "Why don't you pack a suitcase of clothes for Bud and one for yourself—and take some clean clothes for Happy. When we get her from the bus we will drive on up to Seattle, spend the night in the Ridpath Hotel, and the next day we will drive on north—visit Banff, Lake Louise, and we'll go on up to Vancouver and over to Victoria Island. We'll just have a vacation."

Well, nothing suited me better, so I got us all ready, and on the appointed day we drove over to Tacoma, got Happy off the camp bus, drove up to Seattle, and checked into the Ridpath Hotel. Now it was time for me to tell Dub that I needed to spend that afternoon finding and buying school shoes for the children. Moses Lake did not have many stores and my children's feet were hard to fit, so I needed to take advantage of having many and larger stores at which to "shop."

There was no way that Dub was going to spend his afternoon in Seattle going in and out of stores looking for shoes for children, so he told me to go on and do the shopping and he would just spend the afternoon walking around town. We would meet back at the hotel in the late afternoon, have dinner, and then possibly go to a picture show. So we went our separate ways.

Late afternoon, we did meet back at the hotel. I showed the shoes I had bought and Dub bragged on them—and then I asked him what he had done. And do you know, he had gone into Merrill Lynch, Pierce, Fenner and Beane, and he had bought twenty shares of Pepsi Cola stock. He had paid $23.87 a share for it, plus a commission of $7.78—a total of $485.18—and that was money I had planned to spend in Canada buying myself some wool sweaters and skirts. Oh, I was furious. You can believe me when I tell you that that man slept in a very cold bed for many, many nights.

Oh, we went on the trip. We stayed in some beautiful hotels built of stone and covered with ivy. They had been built by Union Pacific Railroad Co. as it made its way across Canada. We had some wonderful meals—and beautiful "teas." I saw real totem poles, carved by real Indians. I saw old men bowling on the green. We saw everything there was to see—but when we returned to Moses Lake my suitcase had in it exactly the clothes that I had packed before we left. I had no money to buy any "junk."

These memories came flooding back to me on that July day in 1990 as I sat reading the letter about the stock split. You see, at Dub's death in 1972 I had decided to sell all the little bits of stock that he owned because I didn't know anything about stock. But when I looked at that Pepsi Cola stock I thought, "You know, old girl, as much as you complained about that stock you should be stuck with it forever." So I didn't sell it. I left it there and I wrote the company and asked them not to ever send me a dividend—just to keep it there and reinvest it. I just did not want to be bothered with anything about Pepsi Cola.

But on that July day I looked down at the letter to see how much stock I owned. It said 443—four hundred and forty-three shares. Why, we had only bought twenty. Then I looked to see how much it was worth for each share—$77.37. Man, it was time for the calculator. I got out the calculator—and do you know that on that day that stock was worth $34,274.91—and it had taken only thirty-five years.

I cast my eyes up to heaven. I was sure that Dub was up there thinking that I was going to say, "Thank you, Dub"—but that is not what I said. When I looked toward heaven what I said was, "Why didn't you buy more?"

A Man to Bank On

CHARLOTTE PUGH BYRN

Unless you grew up in a small town and had a very old father, you probably wouldn't know how things were then and there. My hometown was small and my father was old. Very old—even for me. Recently, President Bush inspired me to tell these stories of my father when he reminded the nation that older people were the living link to the past.

I listen to talk radio—as a matter of fact, I call talk radio—but on June 27, 1990, I was listening—not calling—and I found out something about myself that I had not known before. I discovered that I am not a lip reader. I found out that throughout the entire presidential campaign of 1988, I had not read George Bush's lips correctly. He was not saying, "No new taxes"—he was saying, "Many new taxes." This shocking revelation was followed by the disastrous news that our country is in terrible fiscal shape. We are broke—and not only that but we owe millions and billions of dollars. As my mind registered this fact I couldn't help but think of my father. I couldn't help but think, "This would never have happened if my father had been running this country." And why did I think this? Let me tell you about my father.

He was born in 1869—four years after the close of the War Between the States, which is the real name of that war that the Yankees have always called the Civil War. His parents were of English–Welsh heritage, and he grew up to be a small town banker in Hamburg, Arkansas. Now if you think that being the banker's daughter made me anything special, you are mistaken. It didn't. What it made me was the bank's janitor. Every morning I went to the bank with my father at opening time—which, incidentally, was about seven o'clock—and I swept the lobby and the front walk. My older brother swept behind the cage. We got paid ten cents a day—which was pretty good wages for those days. We also swept the Presbyterian Church, but we had to do that for nothing—that was what we owed the Lord.

Now, my father's bank was not a bank for lending money—it was a bank for saving money. My mother always said that you could get a kinder look out of a glass eye than you could from my father if you went in to borrow money. I think she was right.

My father would lend you money for only four reasons. You could borrow if someone in your family was sick and you needed to take them to the hospital. You could borrow if someone in your family died and you needed to bury him. You could borrow to make a crop, or you could borrow to educate a child. Now, I thought he would always lend money for those reasons but on a recent visit to my old home town I found out that this was not true. A friend of mine told me of an experience one of *his* friends had.

His friend, one of the Ross boys, had gone into the bank one spring to borrow money to make his crop. Sure enough, that year the weather was right; there were no army worms or boll weevils; and he made a good crop. Well, the price of cotton was "up," so he made lots of money. As soon as he sold his crop, he went into the bank and with part of the money he paid off his note. With the rest of the money, he went over to Mr. Searcy Wilcoxon's Chevrolet place and bought himself an automobile.

Well, the next spring he went into the bank to borrow money for that year's crop. My friend said that my father looked at him over his glasses and said, "Bud, I hear you bought an automobile."

"Yessir, I did," said the Ross boy proudly.

"Well," my father continued, "you bring me the four wheels off that automobile and let me lock them in the vault and I'll lend you the money. Otherwise, no—there is no way in the world that you can make a crop if you are riding around in that automobile."

My friend said that was the year the Ross boy quit farming and began running a jitney.

My father believed in work. As a matter of fact, I worked far beyond the age of normal retirement because he led me to believe that if I didn't work I couldn't *eat*. I really think that he thought I should not even breathe if I wasn't working.

He got up early. He had a little verse he used to say to us:

> *He who would thrive*
> *Must get up at five.*
> *He who would thrive more*
> *Must get up at four.*
> *But he who would thrive the most of all*
> *Must never go to sleep at all.*

He also went to bed early at night. I never did know whether this was because he was tired or if it was because if he was in bed with the lights out he was saving on electricity.

Not only did my father save *his* money, he believed that everyone else should save theirs. After I was married and living at home during World War II, I would honestly wait until he came home for dinner—which we ate at twelve o'clock—and then rush down to the bank to cash a check. Invariably, if he was there, he would try to talk me into drawing out less. If I wrote the check for ten dollars he would say, "Honey, don't you think five would be enough?" And this was *my* money. Why once, when Miss Genie Dew bought a car—and gave a check for it—she avoided my father for several weeks, knowing that he would get after her for buying that new car. Her old one was good enough—he thought.

One evening, after the birth of one of my children, I was, as was customary in those times, rocking her to sleep and singing her a lullaby. I was softly singing, "Bye baby, bye. Bye baby, bye."

My father walked into the room and stopped at once, as if frozen—and said, "Honey, don't sing 'Bye baby, bye' to that child. You sing 'Save baby, save.'"

I did, but that baby, now grown, buys a lot, so I know it didn't work.

My father never went to an ophthalmologist. I'm not even sure that specialty existed during his life. When he needed new glasses he just went into Mr. Baker's store, stood at the counter and tried on glasses until he found the pair through which he could see best. Now, I started not to mention that for fear you would think we were crude—but recently I visited an ophthalmologist. I was escorted into the office by a nice young lady in a pretty little uniform. She sat me down in a very elaborate chair. Soon the doctor arrived in his nice uniform and put a large machine down in front of my face. He covered one eye, then he placed a piece of clear glass in front of the other eye, left it there a second or two, removed it and place a different piece of clear glass in front of that same eye. Then he said to me, "Now, which one did you see the best through?" Well, that is exactly what my father did standing at the counter in Baker's store.

Every time I go to Ashley County to visit I hear new stories about my father. On a recent trip the whole town was excited because they were preparing to celebrate Scottie Pippin Day. You see, Scottie Pippin, one of the best players on the Chicago Bulls basketball team, graduated from Hamburg High School. So of course I heard a story about my father and Mr. Prink P. Pippin, Scottie's great-grandfather.

Mr. Prink Pippin had his farm in Ashley County so close to the Louisiana line that if he went out his front gate he stepped into Louisiana—but his farm was behind his house so it was in Ashley County, Arkansas. Mr. Pippin did his ginning and banking up in Hamburg. It seems that one year he went into the bank to get a loan to make his crop. My father welcomed him and said, "Come on in, Prink, and let's fix up this mortgage so I can sleep nights." Well, they fixed up the mortgage, and Mr. Pippin left with his money. A few days later, Mr. Pippin came into the bank and returned the money. When he was questioned as to why he was returning the loan he replied, "Mr.

Pugh, when you fixed that mortgage so that *you* could sleep, you fixed it so that I couldn't."

Maybe those days are gone forever. Maybe forevermore our country and its citizens will be in debt. Maybe my father was just one of a kind. I don't know about that, but I do know this: forty years after his death, in the little town of Hamburg, Arkansas, people are still telling their children and their grandchildren about Mr. Frank N. Pugh. He will be long remembered and often quoted by everyone who ever knew him.

BRUCE DAVIS

TED COLSON is a Professor Emeritus at the University of North Texas, where he taught storytelling. In his time at UNT, he helped pioneer the storytelling movement in Texas, and he is a noted scholar on oral history collection. He has been a presenter and storyteller for several storytelling conferences and for national and regional communication association conventions. He is a co-founder of both the Tejas Storytelling Association and the Texas Story-telling Festival. A teller at the first-ever Texas Storytelling Festival, he is known throughout the state for his personal remembrance tales.

The Story of Mahsuri

TED COLSON

This story was told to me by Salamah Mohamed-Ismail. Salamah was from the city of Ipoh, the state of Perak, in western Malaysia. The locale of the story is the island of Langwaki which is near Ipoh. Salamah reported that the story appears in print but is often told by word-of-mouth to children. Everyone in Malaysia knows the story, since it is an integral part of that country's folk literature. Sadly, soon after the interview that produced this story, Salamah died in an automobile accident in Colorado.

Long ago, on the island of Langwaki in western Malaysia, there lived a young woman of royal blood named Mahsuri. She was a beautiful woman and very well known and loved by the people. When she was of age, she married a handsome and good man. He was a prosperous merchant who was trusted by the king. Soon after the marriage, the husband was sent across the seas to sell goods for the king. Since his journey was to last a very long time, the husband asked his good friend to watch over Mahsuri and keep her safe, and the good friend agreed to do so.

Now, there was another young man who was extremely jealous. He had loved Mahsuri for a very long time, and he was angry that she had married the merchant instead of himself. When he realized that the husband was gone on a long sea voyage and that the good friend was entrusted with Mahsuri's care, the jealous man saw an opportunity to take revenge on Mahsuri and her husband.

At that time it was not legal for a man and a woman who were not married to be in the same house alone. When the jealous man realized that the good friend came frequently to Mahsuri's house to see to her welfare, he saw his chance to create a false story and thereby take revenge on Mahsuri. He told everyone that the good friend was seeing Mahsuri alone and that they were lovers. The gossip spread rapidly, and soon everyone heard the story and many believed it. The king witnessed all of these things, and he realized that he had to take steps to punish the two. In the meantime, the jealous man sent a letter to Mahsuri's husband telling him that he must return because Mahsuri had been unfaithful to him.

41

A day was set for the punishment. All the time Mahsuri denied that she had done wrong, but it was decreed that Mahsuri was to be put to death. When the day arrived for her execution Mahsuri told the king and the people that they would see that she was innocent. She told them that if she were guilty her blood would run red; but, if she were innocent her blood would be white. She also prophesied that if she was wrongly executed that for seven generations the island would be poor and that even though the land was good, no one would be able to cultivate anything on it. Nevertheless, Mahsuri's gruesome execution was ordered. She was killed by a long sword that was placed into her mouth and forced down her throat into her body. Instantly, Mahsuri's blood ran white as snow. Everyone knew that she was innocent and that a terrible injustice had been committed.

It was true, just as Mahsuri predicted: for seven generations the land turned fallow and the island was not good for cultivation. As a result the people became very poor and suffered greatly. One year the island was invaded by the Siamese army and they burned the rice fields. The entire area was burned so that the rice turned black. It is said that even to this day one can find grains of blackened, burned rice in the sands.

But the seven generations have passed. The eighth generation from the time of Mahsuri how inhabits the island of Langwaki, and life is much, much better. But the people still tell the story of the terrible wrong that was committed when the beautiful and innocent Mahsuri was killed. Even though the people are now properous, they do not forget the long years of suffering that their own bad judgment brought upon them.

Dad Watches the Moonwalk

TED COLSON

Are you old enough to remember where you were on Sunday night, July 20, 1969? If you don't remember that exact date, maybe you will remember where you were the night Neil Armstrong walked on the moon.

That's one of those memorable events that gets permanently etched in your memory. Like the day President Kennedy was shot, or, if you have been around a really long time, the day FDR died, or the day Pearl Harbor was attacked.

Most adults remember the night of the moonwalk and can tell you exactly where they were and with whom they were watching. It is especially vivid for me because of the circumstances in which I found myself.

I like to collect family stories, and that night, quite serendipitously, I got one of my favorites.

My father and I watched the first moonwalk together. On that day he was visiting my home. He was eighty-two years old at the time. My mother had died only weeks before, and all my siblings and I were very protective of him—trying to see to it that he was happy as possible and trying to help him adjust to being alone after sixty-two years of marriage.

All that day we looked forward to the big moment. Dad was excited about it all. In mid-afternoon we heard those words: "The Eagle has landed." And we both became more excited at the promise that in a few hours we would see a live telecast of Armstrong walking on the moon.

We spent a pleasant evening together during which time Dad had one or two of his favorite libation—bourbon and water.

Then just before ten o'clock that night we sat awestruck, like most Americans, as we saw Armstrong actually step onto the surface of the moon and heard him make his historic statement: "That's one small step for a man, one giant leap for mankind."

Our silence was finally broken when my dad said, "My, my, can you believe this. Here I am, I've lived long enough to see a man walk on the moon, and to think that my daddy brought me from Tennessee to Indian Territory in a wagon. Uh, uh. Doesn't seem possible."

That did seem incredible. But then I remembered that only recently I had read that his generation, those born in the late nineteenth century and living into the post-World War II era, had seen more changes in their world than any other generation in the history of mankind. I realized, that's my dad they're talking about!

I said, "Its hard for me to even imagine that you actually made that long journey in a wagon. Do you remember anything about that move from Tennessee to Indian Territory?"

And he began:

"Lordy, no, I can't remember. I wasn't but about four years old. All I remember is what Papa and your Aunt Cora and Ella told me of it."

"As I understand it, Papa and Mama were married in Clarksville, Tennessee, where he was born. They were both fairly young when they got married. My mother, as you know, was an Indian or at least had Indian blood, and that was not something to be proud of back in those days, so neither of their families much approved of their getting married. But they did. And they got along, I guess, for a while. Started a family and all.

"I guess Papa finally decided that he could do better if he went west. I guess he just left his wife—my mama—and his family, and came over here to what was then Indian territory to try his luck. I don't know how long they were separated that way—maybe a couple of years. He settled in Ardmore, which was kind of booming at that time. And he opened a livery stable. It caught on real quick and he was pretty successful at it.

"After he got his business going, I guess, is when he went back to Tennessee to get his family—Mama and us kids. I suppose that would be your Aunt Ella, your Aunt Cora, and me—since Cora and Ella were older than me. Anyhow, after he got things settled in Tennessee, he loaded us all up and we started back to Ardmore in a wagon. I understand he brought a colored woman along with him to help him take care of the family and especially to look after Mama, since she was pregnant again.

"Anyway, they made it along pretty good until they got somewhere around Paris, Texas. Then is when Mama went into labor, I guess, or was suffering somehow. I never knew if it was because the baby was due, or if she was about to have a miscarriage, or whatever. But, anyhow, Papa decided they had to stop and do something.

"They came upon what appeared to be a farmhouse—Ella always said she remembered it to be a log house. Anyhow, Papa pulled in and found that nobody was there. It was deserted. He got that colored woman busy taking care of my mother and started unloading things they would be needing.

"It wasn't any time until some man rode up. Probably saw chimney smoke where he had started a fire or something like that. But this man rode up with a shotgun and he told Papa that it was his place and that they couldn't stay there. Papa told him what the situation was and that come hell or high water they were going to stay there 'til his wife was able to travel again. That man wasn't too happy about things, but I guess he saw that there wasn't much to do about it. So he told Papa that he could stay the night, but he wanted him to get on his way the next day.

"I don't know how long it was, or what was going on, but as I understand it sometime in the night, or sometime the next day, or maybe it was two or three days, I don't know, but finally, both my Mama and that baby died. Like I say, I don't know if it was because the baby came too early, or what, but, anyhow, both of them died.

"Well, what could Papa do? He had both Mama and that baby buried together somewhere in or around Paris, Texas. I always understood that they were buried together in some cemetery in town, but I will never know."

After a somewhat long silence, I said, "Dad, that's a remarkable story. And sad. Does it ever bother you that you don't know much about where your mother is buried, or any of the other details?"

He said, "Well, years later, your mother and I tried to see what we could find out about my mama's grave. We wrote to Paris—to the county record-keepers, you know. We wrote two or three letters back and forth, but it didn't do much good. In those days there weren't very good records kept, so who knows …"

After another pause, he ended his story by saying, "Oh, I guess it would be a kind of satisfaction to know where she's laid. But I never knew her, I mean I don't remember her, and so I can't grieve. Anyhow, I suppose that kind of thing happened to a lot of families trying to move west in those days. And you know, I'll bet there are a lot of good women buried along the way."

45

The Legend of the Rainbow

TED COLSON

Aim-Ora Bunnag is a young woman from Thailand who enrolled as a graduate student at the University of North Texas. While in attendance, she took a course from me that involved group performance of literature. One assignment required each student to select a short story and adapt it for performance by multiple voices. Ms. Bunnag asked if she could use a Thai folk story. I was delighted with her choice. Following is the story as Aim-Ora originally told it and which she later adapted for group performance.

Long, long ago, when the earth was still new, it had no colors. There were no differences in the ocean and the sky. There was no difference anywhere. There was a great "sameness" about all the things on the earth. The people who lived then were very bored with their lives. There was nothing around them that was special and they were all like machines—they would wake up, work, eat, and sleep. The only difference they knew was the black of night and the light of day. And so, they went about their dreary jobs, day after day. They knew that if they did not plow, they would not have rice to eat. They knew that if they did not grow cotton, they would have no cloth to make their clothes. So, they went on living like a big machine. They got up, worked, ate, and slept. They had work to do, but the were very bored. No one even thought about the possibility of change. No one, that is, except Nuan.

Nuan was a charming little girl, and she had a wonderful imagination! Sometimes the people chastised her when she talked about her imaginary things and about her wonderful dreams. They thought she was very foolish. As you know, adults don't like little girls like Nuan. Proper little children must obey their parents and listen to the adults' words and thoughts and must help their families with the work that must be done.

Nuan was not a naughty girl. She did the things that were assigned to her as her duties, but sometimes—often, in fact—she thought about changes. One day, after a hard day's work helping her mother pick cotton, she slept and dreamed.

Now, there was a very kind angel—a blue angel—who always looked after Nuan. When the blue angel saw that Nuan was crying, she slipped into Nuan's dream and into her mind.

"Young lady," said the blue angel, "why are you crying?"

And Nuan said, "I am bored. I do not want to live in a boring world."

And the blue angel said, "Why do you find the world boring?"

Nuan answered, "Don't you see? This blank world. This empty world where there is nothing special. Everything goes on as it has always gone. We all have to do the same things at the same times every day and every night, day in and day out. I want a change."

And the angel said, "What kind of change would you have, my dear?"

"Oh, something different," said Nuan. "Something lively—different. The sky, the sea, the trees, everything—they are the same. They are—oh, how can I tell you?"

The angel smiled and said, "Color! You want the world to be painted with different colors, like this ..." The angel waved her hand, and a rainbow came into the sky.

"Yes," said Nuan. "Color! That is exactly the change we need. Color!"

Because the blue angel learned of the humans' need through Nuan's dream, she decided to forsake the joy of being an angel and come to paint the earth with herself and by herself.

One day the kind blue angel went to the chief angel and asked, "Has any angel ever asked to leave heaven?"

The chief angel was amazed. She had never heard such a question, for it is certain that no one ever wanted to leave heaven—the wonderland.

"Leave here?" asked the chief angel. "What are you talking about? Who would ever want to leave this colorful and joyful place?"

But an unexpected thing was about to happen. The kind blue angel asked the chief angel, "Would you be so kind as to let me go to the earth?"

"Have I really heard you correctly?" asked the chief angel. "Do you really mean that you would leave this wonderful place?"

The blue angel answered, "Yes. I want to go. I want to go to earth. I cannot bear to see the poor humans, whom I love, living in their colorless and boring world. I would like to paint the earth—or at least the sky. Since I am a blue angel I can only be one color. Please give me your blessing, and I will do that which calls me."

The chief angel said, "Oh, my dear. We will miss you very much."

And the blue angel said, "I know, but I have to go even though I very much enjoy being here. I sympathize with those poor humans below. Please let me go. If you miss me, you can look around the sky and I will always be there."

"Bless you," said the chief angel and allowed the little blue angel to depart.

The blue angel became blue pigment and drifted across the sky. The north wind helped her blow herself across the sky, and her blue color covered all the atmosphere of the earth.

The next morning, as the day was just beginning, everyone got up as usual to start their day's work.

"My, my," said an old man, "what a soft sunlight there is today."

"Yes," said another, "and feel the soft wind, too."

Still a third one said, "Right. The sun shines so gently today. What has happened?"

They all felt better than they had ever felt before, but they did not know why. No one had bothered to look up at the sky.

Perhaps the little blue angel was too sensitive. When she saw that no one noticed the beautiful sky she had painted, she began to cry. Her teardrops fell as rain and combined with the waters of the earth. And her tears colored the seas. They, too, turned a beautiful blue, and the little girl Nuan saw it.

"Look!" said Nuan. "My dream is coming true!"

"Go back to your work, girl, or you will be beaten by your mother," said an old man.

But Nuan didn't hear him. "My dream is coming true!" she said. "We have color! Look at the sea! Look at the beautiful sky above!"

"What is she doing?" someone asked.

"Oh, it's just that naughty girl, Nuan. She is just being foolish again."

"Sounds like she is trying to tell us something."

"Pay no attention. It's something foolish she's talking about, as usual. Nuan, come here. Don't run in the rain. Come here."

But Nuan again said, "Look at the sea. Look at the sky. The rain has stopped and the sun is shining. Look. Everyone, come out of your houses and see!"

The rain had stopped and the sun was shining, and a great and wonderful thing occurred. Seven colored stripes ran across the sky all the way to the ground. Happiness was in everyone's heart.

"Look, everyone," said Nuan. "Look at the beautiful sky and sea. Look at the beautiful stripes in the sky."

"I don't believe it," said a little old woman. "Why, it's wonderful!"

"The colors!" said Nuan. "They have come into our world. My dream has come true."

And then everyone began to notice the changes, and all began to voice their wonder:

"What has happened to the tree? The trunk is dark ..."

"But the leaves are green."

"Look at the flowers. There are many colors."

"That is violet, that is blue ..."

"That's green, yellow, orange, red."

"Look! The corn is green and yellow!"

"Look at the cow. The colors join together. It is brown."

"Have you ever seen anything as beautiful as this?"

"No. And it is not an illusion. It is real. Oh, I have never been as happy as this."

And so, everyone looked with astonishment at the beautiful things around them. And they were very happy. They knew that from that time forward, they would have a wonderful life in a vividly colored world.

And we shouldn't forget that the seven angels who followed the blue angel—the ones who colored the rainbow—were also very, very pleased to see the people of the new, colorful world so happy. And to this day, the seven angels appear after the rain to sing and dance with the sky, and to assure the people of the world that they will always be there and that the people will always have a beautiful, colorful world.

BRIAN KANOF

ALLEN DAMRON *is* Texas. He bounds onto the stage with a grin that says he intends to have at least as good a time as the audience, carrying a guitar he can almost hide behind. Known for his musical performances of everything from classical to folk music, he is also a gifted storyteller. He began to earnestly incorporate stories into his musical sets after his first performance at the Texas Storytelling Festival in 1990. He has ranged outside the United States to Canada, England, France, and Italy, and is one of only nine performers officially designated by the Texas legislature as goodwill ambassadors from the State of Texas to the world. He lives in Austin, Texas.

The Cook of El Rancho Cultural

ALLEN DAMRON

As a native Texan, stories of the cowboy and ranching life have always appealed to me. Some of it I have even lived. For decades, I traveled around the world sharing the real Texas through song. A few years ago, I was invited to share songs and ballads at the Texas Storytelling Festival. The experience awakened the true storyteller within me. Tales from El Rancho Cultural were among my first.

Recently we found out that Cookie matriculated—that's what he said—from a place called Harvard Law School. We figured he must have done somethin' real bad to serve that many years. We figured it must have been worse than when Shorty was arrested for DWI with a whole pickup load of sotol for our Fourth of July celebration. He spent ten days in jail, then had to go to Defensive Driving School for some more days.

We felt sorry for Cookie for havin' to learn all them laws, and not just driving laws. But out here a man don't ask what you done to deserve that kind of punishment. We just take you as you are—and go forward. Whatever Cookie had done, he has paid his debt to society.

You see, out here at El Rancho Cultural, a man's own bidness is his own bidness. Everbody leaves Cookie alone, 'ceptin' the times he makes frog legs. Now I've got a lot of respect for something that still tries to hop out of the pan and escape after it's been cut in two and fried. Well, frogs is easy to come by down by the stock tank. Late in the evenin', with a .22 rifle, you can fill a tow sack in about an hour. Unfortunately, you can also fill a No. 2 washtub with rattlesnakes in about the same time, cuz rattlers like frogs better than us. (And they wonder why cowboys wear boots!)

So, Cookie came up with an idea. "Let's go 'em one better. Since they's bound to be more frogs than rattlesnakes in France, and the rattlers have been eatin' the frogs, it means that we is a little further up the food chain by eatin' rattlesnakes." Well, since we'd been dodgin', shootin', cussin', and generally trying to annihilate the breed all of our lives, it had never occured to us to cook one of them. Now we had done had some frogs and they was pretty good—it was kinda like chicken, but different. So we figured that we'd have a real leg up on gourmet eatin' (Cookie told me to say, "Excuse

51

the pun," but I ain't kicked a football since I was in high school. Well, anyway, I digress...)

So with a great degree of trepidation—Cookie says to use that word cuz it's real cultural, and I ain't got a notion what it means—I sets forth to slay the mighty rattlesnake for a real Texas gourmet meal. As luck would have it, I killed two of the largest rattlers I've ever seen, about a hundred yards from each other—they's both over seven feet. So I says if this don't feed the bunkhouse, nothin' will. I drive back in triumph with two rattlesnakes big around as my leg, throws them to Cookie and says, "Cook 'em up." He looks at 'em, shakes his head, and says, "Couldn't you have gotten some younger ones?" I says, "They don't *fillet* near as good and besides, rattlesnake is rattlesnake."

That evenin' we sat down to a meal with a couple of old enemies. Cookie had made some hollandaise sauce—Cookie explained that Holland is real close to France, it's like from here to Lubbock—and it turned out great. If they'd feed more of their frogs to them rattlers in France, they'd eat a whole lot better—a little culinary advice from El Rancho Cultural.

Well, it wasn't too long before we all got to worrying that Cookie had to spend so many years going to that law school, that the boss might fire him—what with being an ex-con and all.

So, when Mrs. Boss's Birthday Bar-B-Q came around, we kinda sidled off to the side and presented the boss with a signed affidavit that we was on Cookie's side, and a more honest man could not be found and a finer pot of pinto beans had not been cooked before.

The boss laughs to bust a gut. And allows as to how Cookie had told him as much in his resume, which is what cowboys write to get a job, and if a horse stomps you in complete the boss will know where to send the back pay and tack ... next-of-kin, they call it. And the newspaper can write something real nice like, "Won the saddle bronc in Mesquite Rodeo five years ago." But I digress ...

The boss said that Cookie's dad had been his lawyer for years, and he had seen Cookie grow up. Now all of us has had some run-in with lawyers, having been divorced an equal amount of times that we had been married. And we had a very low opinion of the breed—ah, lawyers that is, not women.

So, when we found out that Cookie had been fully trained to be a lawyer, and instead had come back to the ranch country to cook for us, we was shore relieved. He had seen the error of his ways and had decided to be an honest man.

ACCENT PHOTOGRAPHY

Known to many as the pioneer of storytelling in Texas, ELIZABETH ELLIS shares a wide range of stories, from Celtic folktales to personal experiences taken from her childhood in the Appalachian Mountains. She was the first recipient of the John Henry Faulk Award and among the featured tellers at the first-ever Texas Storytelling Festival. She is one of a handful of tellers who have been invited to perform more than five times at the National Storytelling Festival. A past president of the Tejas Storytelling Association, she currently serves on the board of directors of the National Storytelling Association. She lives in Dallas with her grandson Christopher.

The Birth of Oisin

ELIZABETH ELLIS

The only Finn McCool story most folks know today is "The Legend of Knockmany."
It is a comic tale that paints Finn as a buffoon. This story is a truer representation
of Finn. I love to tell it because it introduces the power and wonder of the entire cycle
of tales about him.

When Connor MacNessa was High King at Tara, and a very good time that was, Finn McCool had just been made leader of the Fianna, Ireland's standing army, but Ireland was at peace. So Finn was at home on the hill of Allen or out in the fields hunting with the men. And one day, as he was hunting, he came into a little clearing, and there was a sight that he had never thought to see. For there were the hunting dogs standing in a ring, barking and baying as they always did. But between them stood Finn's own dogs, Bran and Skolaun, and they bared their teeth and held the other dogs at bay. For between Bran and Skolaun there stood a red roe deer.

That was a great wonder, so Finn walked toward the deer. It seemed to have no fear of him. It even let him put his hand on its head. So when the men came, Finn bade them leash their dogs. And when Finn returned to the hill of Allen, as always, behind him ran Bran and Skolaun. But this night, behind them there followed the red roe deer. And that night, when Finn sat at the table for his meat, below him as always lay Bran and Skolaun. But this night, between them lay the red roe deer, and it licked Finn McCool's hand.

Late that night Finn awoke with the sure and certain knowledge that someone was standing in his room. When he was fully awake, before him there was the most beautiful woman he had ever seen. She had big brown eyes and long auburn hair that tumbled down her back. She said, "I am Sav, daughter of Bov the Red, and I was the red roe deer that followed you home from the hunt."

Finn said, "Lady, how can that be?"

She replied, "I am loved by one of the Dark Immortals, but because I could not return his love, he touched me with his Druid wand and changed me into the shape of the red roe deer. Another old Druid took pity on me and told me if I could gain sanctuary here on the hill of Allen that I would regain my own shape again. So, I have come to you."

Finn gathered all the covers of his couch about him and stood up. He said, "Lady, you are right welcome here. Stay as long as ever you like." He made her a room of cedar and lapis and she lived in it. As time went on, Finn went less and less into the fields to hunt with the men and stayed more and more at home on the hill of Allen, until finally he and Sav were married.

One day, as they sat at the table for their meat, a runner came to Finn McCool from Connor MacNessa saying that the longboats had been seen off Ireland's shore once more. Finn must bring the Fianna to defend her. When Sav heard this, she began to weep. But Finn said, "Don't cry. The love I have for you will lend wings to my feet. I'll be back before you even know that I am gone. Watch for me from the ramparts. You'll soon see me coming home to you." But she wept the more at his leaving.

Every day she would climb to the top of the ramparts and look far down the hill of Allen, hoping for the sight of that red-gold hair gleaming in the sun, or for the sight of Bran and Skolaun, outracing their master, headed home. One day, as she looked far down the hill of Allen, it seemed to her that the sun was gleaming off something. When it came nearer, she could see that it was bright red-gold hair.

With a cry of joy on her lips, she ran through the gateway and down the hill. But when she neared the figure, her heart dropped, for she could see that though it had the look of Finn about it, it did not have the feel of Finn. She grew frightened and turned to run back. But strange dogs cut her off from the gate. Before her the shape changed, and there stood the Dark Immortal, who reached out and touched her with his Druid wand. And once more she took the shape of the red roe deer.

When the servants saw what was happening, they grabbed up any weapons that came to hand and came running out the door to defend their mistress. But now there was nothing there. Torn-up grass. A vast emptiness. And far off at the foot of the hill of Allen the distant sound of hounds baying at the hunt.

When Finn came home, no one wanted to tell the tale. But like all evil stories, at last it was told. When Finn had heard it, he went into his chamber and slammed the door. He sat there for four days and nights speaking to no one. At the end of the fourth day, he came out and whistled up Bran and Skolaun and left the hill of Allen, searching for Sav. The length and breadth of Ireland he sought her. At the end of seven years of searching, he returned once more to the hill of Allen and took up the leadership of the Fianna. But there was no music on Allen now. There was never any laughter.

One day, when he was out in the fields, he came into a little clearing, and there was that sight that he had thought he would never see again. For there was the circle of hunting dogs who barked and bayed as they always did. Once more Bran and Skolaun stood in the midst of them and bared their teeth and held the other dogs at bay. But between Bran and Skolaun this time there was not a red roe deer. Between them now there stood a small sturdy boy with bright red-gold hair. He looked to be about six or seven years of age. The child was mother naked and seemed not to have the habit of human speech.

Finn walked toward the child. The boy showed no fear of him. He even let Finn put his hand on his head. When the men came, Finn bade them leash their dogs. That night when Finn returned to the hill of Allen, as always, behind him followed Bran and Skolaun. But on his shoulders rode the small boy with the bright red-gold hair.

As was the custom of his people, Finn asked the child no question until a year and a day was fully past. And when it was, he called the boy to him, and placing him on his lap, he asked, "Tell me, is there anything you can remember of the time before I brought you here?"

The boy said, "I remember only living in a little glen with a red roe deer and being happy. One day a dark man came and touched her with a long stick and she followed after him. I cried out and tried to go with her, but I fell to the ground and found I could not move. After that I remember little except the searching for her, and the weeping, until you found me and brought me here."

Finn said, "That red roe deer was Sav, daughter of Bov the Red, my wife and your mother. And I will call you Oisin, which in the Old Tongue means Little Fawn."

Oisin grew to be a warrior and a leader among the Fianna in his own right. He was also a singer, a poet, and a storyteller. It is through him that all the tales of Finn McCool come down to us, even to this very day. For Oisin sang sweeter than any man who ever drew breath, so sweet that the gods themselves grew jealous. But that's another story.

Defender of the First Amendment, noted author, television host, "Hee-Haw" cast member—JOHN HENRY FAULK was all of these. History will remember him as the man who, in the 1950s, single-handedly took on McCarthyism and won, who battled against those who conducted witch hunts in the name of freedom, who endured and carved out a place as a champion of free speech. But to the people of Texas, the memory of John Henry Faulk brings to mind another man: a gifted public speaker, a folksy but sophisticated yarnspinner who advanced the art of storytelling and set the standard for personal narratives within that genre. He told at the Texas Storytelling Festival in 1988, in what was to be one of his final appearances anywhere. Annually since 1986, the Tejas Storytelling Association has bestowed the John Henry Faulk Award to individuals who have made outstanding contributions to the art of storytelling. A national treasure and a Texas legend, John Henry Faulk left this world a far better place. (*Photograph by Theresa DiMenno. From the John Henry Faulk Papers, courtesy of The Center for American History, The University of Texas at Austin.*)

Miss Fanny Rollins of Pear Orchard, U.S.A.

JOHN HENRY FAULK

At our third annual festival, John Henry took the stage to accept a proclamation in his honor commemorating our annual John Henry Faulk Award. He spoke of the characters populating both the real and ficticious towns of his own Texas youth. For it was Faulk's conviction that the small towns of America contain the roots of our complex urban world, that they are a microcosm of our larger hopes and fears, and that their inhabitants are pure representations of the national character— demonstrated here by the gossip of Miss Fanny Rollins.

Near from back where I'm from, there's a small town known as Pear Orchard. Actually, there's nothing much to Pear Orchard, it's just an ordinary little town. It's located somewhere between El Paso and Texarkana. The Chamber of Commerce down there has a motto: *Pear Orchard, U.S.A.— the biggest little town in the country.*

Some people might say, "Well, it's a typical town of the Silent Majority." It might be typical of the majority, but there ain't nothing silent about it. The first time I ever visited the place, I found a new friend while looking for a rocking chair. The local furniture store clerk told me they didn't stock rockers anymore but said if I would drive out to see Miss Fanny Rollins, she might have one that she had no more use for.

When I arrived at her mailbox, I could see a long, oleander-bordered walkway leading up to the front porch of a country farm home. A woman was sitting in a porch swing taking up room for four people. That capacious soul was spread all over the swing, her arms resting on her ample bosom, which went all the way around to her backbone, just like a hen fixing to fly off a low roof. I said, "How do, ma'am. I'm looking for Miss Fanny Rollins."

"Heh, heh. Well, honey," she said, "you'd better get an eye doctor if you can't see her. I've been accused of a heap of things, but being invisible ain't one of them. Have a chair, sit down ... That little rocker? ... Yes, it is a nice one ... No, I wouldn't be interested in selling it ... Oh, no. It's funny you mention it, because my daughter-in-law Bertha Mae, Gervis's wife, was over here the other day asking for it. Of course, I can't set in it at all, now. It would take three of them to hold me.

"Bertha Mae's a sweet girl. And talented! Folks don't know it, but bless her heart, she can rub her stomach and pat her head and recite all the books of the Bible backwards. And stop right in the middle to whistle a spiritual. Even preachers can't do that. All her family was talented that way.

"Her oldest brother, Fred, he's one-armed. I don't know how he lost his arm, it was either in a haybaler or a car accident, but I know it was an accident. He didn't do it on purpose. He had a 1952 pickup truck and a double hernia and he could train dogs like nobody I seen. Had that old blue-tick hound named Scooter. Scooter was three-legged, and ever so often people would say, 'I wonder why God left that dog's hind leg off him?'

"God has a purpose. Most dogs, you know, have to slow down to smell around a bush. Well, Scooter scarcely had to pause. He'd do his business and be gone. Fred had him trained to carry a milk bucket. Fred, being one-armed, couldn't pack two buckets of milk at the same time, so Scooter carried the other. Wouldn't spill a drop. Fred had him trained to where he would say, 'Scooter! The wood box is empty,' and Scooter would get up, go trotting out to that woodpile on three legs, pick up a mouthful of kindling, and come drop it in the wood box.

"You know, it's a funny thing, I give Scooter a heap of credit, but not for good judgment when it comes to dynamite and wood. There was a road construction crew working out there one day and Scooter came trotting in with a stick of dynamite. Dropped it in the wood box. And Fred, absent-minded-like, stuck it in the stove.

"I'll say this, it was as interesting a funeral as we ever had here. Never found nothing but Fred's left shoe, and his foot was still in it. The family went down to Cartwright's Funeral Parlor and asked for a left-foot coffin. Cartwright said they didn't stock them. Well, they argued back and forth for the longest time and the family finally settled for buying the whole coffin. I thought it was amusing to see—a coffin big enough for a whole corpse, with just a left foot in it.

"All of that family was talented like that. Take that little old Annie Lee. Oh, that was a sweet thing. But she had a lot of tragedy. When she was about thirteen years old, she went out to the barn to milk the cows and there come up a thunderstorm. Lightning struck her right between the eyes. It soured both buckets of milk. Electricity is strange. It give that child a terrible headache. They thought at first that's all it did, but it turned out to have straightened her hair.

"Oh, bless her little old heart, she tried to get it curly again. She put it up in paper curlers and left it up for thirty-six days in a row as a trial run. She took the curlers out, run her comb through it, and it was straight as a horse's tail. Course that ain't all lightning will do to you—it flattened that child's chest. Well, honey, I ain't talking about being just flat-chested, she was ironing-board flat-chested.

"But she went to town and got her a job working at the state highway department. Saved her money and bought her a pair of foam-rubber bosoms. Oh, it changed her whole outlook on life—from the front. Annie Lee got to where she'd come to church twice on Sunday. Even started singing in the Methodist choir, and she had no more voice than a white leghorn pullet.

"It was all because of the bosoms. And she started coming to our quilting parties every Friday. We had a little old Methodist preacher named Brother Walker, he'd stand there while we quilted, hoorahing with us ladies. Annie Lee was setting at the frame behind me. Brother Walker, he was laughing and chatting, and all of a sudden his jaw went slack, sweat popped out on his brow, and his eyes rolled back in his head. I thought he was having a fainting spell. I said, 'Brother Walker, are you well?' He didn't answer me at all, he just grabbed the doorknob and went through the door mumbling, 'Oh Lord, oh Lord.' I turned my eyes and seen the occasion for the whole thing. Annie Lee was using that left bosom as a pincushion. She'd run that big Number Nine needle clear through from one side to the other.

"Annie Lee kept on using those bosoms until she found Totsie Taylor and married him. But she still had a lot of tragedy, honey. Totsie was a-setting on the railroad tracks one day, just a-thinking of something, when the *Katy Flyer* came by at seven hundred miles an hour and hit him. Well, I say hit him. It exploded him. He was setting there one minute and the next he was a puff of mist floating across the field. They estimated his remainders floated over two and a half acres. The family leased about four acres for the funeral, just to be safe. The pallbearers all had a turn at the plow. Brother Culpepper came from the Liberty Hill and said it was the biggest funeral he ever preached. Acreage-wise.

"Brother Culpepper always knowed the right thing to say. You know, he preached Papa's funeral. Papa passed away sitting in that little rocker that you're in right now. He had such a quiet passing, I didn't know he was gone, to tell the truth. One afternoon, I was shelling black-eyed peas in my lap. Just a-chatting and a-talking to him and he'd grunt every once in a while. After a while, I didn't notice him a-grunting. I looked up, and he was gone. No death rattle, no struggle. His head just dropped forward. Drop your head forward, honey ... Now let it hang down ... There, just like that. I've always said I ain't no scientist, but if that had been a straight chair, Papa would have come out of it and I would have knowed he was dead. Straight chair won't hold a corpse. But Papa's body just rocked back in that little rocker. That's the reason, honey, I wouldn't sell it for anything in the world. It's got sentimental value to it."

David and Goliath

JOHN HENRY FAULK

More than just a biblical reference, the tale of David and Goliath is a metaphor for the battles that John Henry fought in his professional life. The story proudly represents both Faulk's fight against censorship in the 1950s and his avid stand for civil rights in the 1960s. Faulk's speech takes on the rhythm and sound of an old gospel preacher, and even on the printed page, you can still feel the power of Faulk's steady beat.

There is one more citizen down in Pear Orchard of whom I am very fond. The Reverend Tanner Franklin lives out on a farm, not far from the area where his folks were freed from bondage. Reverend Tanner Franklin is six and a half feet tall, farms all week, and preaches on Sunday in the old Shiloh Baptist Church, a tiny little church down under the cypress trees in the bottomlands along the river.

Reverend Tanner Franklin can't read or write. But he has leaned his ear over close to the earth and has caught the rhythms and the sounds of the earth. There's not a wild bird that nests in all that area that he can't identify by its song. There's not a wildflower that blossoms in his fields that Reverend Tanner Franklin can't hold up to his nose and give its folk name.

Reverend Tanner Franklin is all the more remarkable because he is one of the few men I've ever encountered who is completely free from those limitations that most of mankind has, namely bigotry and prejudice. He is too big for that, has too spacious a soul.

And on the Sunday night I'd like for you to meet him, the congregation of some eighteen to twenty people were gathered by the light of a single lantern hanging from the cross beam over the pulpit, singing an old song. And this old song went:

> *You've got to stand up, you've got to stand up,*
> *You've got to stand up to get the job did.*
> *You've got to stand up, you've got to stand up,*
> *You've got to stand up, you gonna move ahead.*

As that old song ebbed and flowed and ebbed and flowed and died away in a long hum, Reverend Tanner Franklin stood up there in the lantern light and said:

Well, glory, church, that's the song I love. It tells just what we got to do in this old world if we're going to make it on through. We got to stand up and move on ahead. We can't just sit here and study about it all the time. Amen.

Well now, church, in the imaginaton of my mind I want to take you all way back yonder to Bible times.

I see over one slope of the hill the Philistine army all gathered up in battle raiment.

Down across a little creek and over yonder slope of the hill was the Israelite army.

They were having a battle, and neither side winning and neither side losing.

You going to say to me, well, why wasn't the Israelite chillun, God's chosen people, prevailing in the battle?

Church, I have to report to you tonight that the Israelite army was led by an old sit-down-and-do-nothin' by the name of King Saul.

He didn't get up to fight God's battle.

He sat there and studied about it all the time.

Well, now, church, in the imagination of my mind, I want to carry you all to a meadowland.

I see the sheeps grazing 'round on the green grass, butterflies and bees visiting with the flowers, mockingbirds singing in the treetops.

And sitting in the shade of a tree was a sweet little shepherd boy named David, playing on his harp, singing psalms to the Lord and minding his daddy's sheep.

Church, I see old man Jesse, Little David's daddy, when he come hobbling out that morning, callin':

"My son David, your mama's fixed up some clean clothes and vittles for your brothers that's fighting down agin those old mean Philistines.

"Chile, would you take them down to 'em?"

Church, I see that obedient shepherd boy David when he got in the buggy,
    Slap the mule across the back and strike out for the battlefield,
    Get off down there at the battlefield and say "Whoa, mule,"
    Hitch the reins around one wheel of the buggy and come crawling out,
    Look over the battlefield, walk up to a big Israelite soldier and say:
    "Cousin So-and-So, I thought you all had a battle going on here. This here don't look like a battleground to me, look more like a Sunday school picnic ground to me. I don't see nary a lick being struck."

Israelite soldier run his arm around little David, he say, "Baby, look across that creek over there, there among the Philistines.

"See that big tall thing stickin' up like a mountaintop?

"Chile, that ain't no mountaintop, that's that old Philistine giant man Goliath.

"He wants to fight the biggest warrior we got, and we ain't got nary a biggest one this morning."

Church, they tell me that morning something started moving in little David's heart.

He stole down there to the tent where old King Saul was sitting there, holding his head in his hands.

He wasn't fighting God's battle, he was sitting there studying about it.

Hummmmmm. Little David stole in there:

"Well, King Saul, if don't nobody else want to fight that giant man Goliath, let me have a go at it.

"He might look like tall timber to you boys,

"But he look like brush to me,

"And I'll chop him off even with the ground this morning."

Church, old King Saul said, "Go ahead on, fight him honey, we're going to lose the war anyhow."

But little David wasn't thinking that way.

He walked down to the creek and selected himself five smooth stones, and all alone and by himself, church—now, mind you—all alone and by himself that chile David started stealing up the slope yonder toward the Philistine army.

Now, hear me, church.

The mightiest force the world had ever seen at that time was all arrayed up yonder amongst the Philistines.

And little David marched on up there,

All alone and by himself,

With just a purpose in his mind.

Old man Goliath was a-marching around there, a-talking big.

Oh, he was a giant man, so many cubits high I can't number them all.

He was carrying a sword in his hand longer than a wagon tongue,

And a shield on his arm bigger than a housetop.

He raised his big old ugly foot up,

And stomped the ground real hard, it shook acorns off the trees 'way over in the next county.

Oh, that giant man spied little David coming up the slope,

And said, "Now who sent a shirttail young 'un to do battle with me?

"Chile, you better turn around and get home to your mama.

64

"I'll step on you and not leave enough for the buzzards to pick."

Up in Zion that morning, church, God got word that His chile David was fighting His battle for Him.

Called the angels together and said:

"Move around heaven and find me a bright rainbow to wear around my neck for a scarf this morning.

"Hush the winds down in the four corners of the Earth.

"Stand the Sun still in the heavens where it's at,

"And some of you angels bend low with your wing tips and sweep the skies clear.

"I want a clear view, a clear view of my chile David,

"Fighting my battle for me down there this morning."

Church, as the Lord and His angels peeked down over the battlements of glory, little David slipped a smooth stone in his slingshot and he started winding up.

Old man Goliath says, "Boy, I told you not to wind that thing up at me that way."

About that time little David caught him right between the eyes with a rock.

Whop!

And that giant man measured his length out on the ground.

The Philistines, seeing it, fled over the hilltops and in fear and trembling dispersed and have not returned since,

Nor been heard of to this day.

Little David walked up there and took that big sword off of that giant man,

And sawed his ugly head off with it.

The Israelite army all came a-running and a-shouting glory

And said, "Little David's a hero!"

But little David said, "No such a thing. All I did is get up and move on ahead.

"God wants them in this world to get up and get the job did,

"Not just sit there and study about it."

Amen.

NICHOLE FORD

Despite making his living as an insurance salesman, JAMES FORD is known for a life full of tall tales. He combines the experiences of growing up in Houston's Fifth Ward with his eclectic and unusual personal observations about modern life. He is known for both his touching family tales and his outrageous lies, and is a four-time grand champion of the Houston Liar's Contest. He is the past president of the Houston Storytellers Guild, and is currently president of the Tejas Storytelling Association. He first told at the Texas Storytelling Festival in 1990.

Johnson and the Red Bandanna

JAMES FORD

This story grew out of a true situation that happened to me many years ago while I was serving in the United States Air Force down in Alexandria, Louisiana. My fishing buddy and I went to our favorite fishing hole, "to fish with lures for the very first time." I caught a rather large black bass, but I was not nearly as unselfish as I appear to be in the story. Quite the contrary, I told my friend not to put his hands on my fish and I didn't need his help with the net he offered. My friend insisted then and now that he saw no fish. The true version of "the one that got away" is as funny to me as the embellished one.

There are a lot of different kinds of friends. But the one I like the best is the one I refer to as a whittling and spitting friend. That's the kind of friend that you just enjoy his company; just whittle and spit and maybe never say a word to one another. A friend like that can sit out in the middle of a lake with you and maybe you never say more than one or two sentences all day, like "Pass the bait" or "Pass a beer." I had a friend like that once. His name was Johnson. Johnson and I used to go fishing all the time. Best I could tell, we'd fish every weekend for a thousand years.

But I remember one time Johnson and I decided to go fishing for the very first time with just lures. I mean we weren't going to use any of those tried, true, and tested fish-catchers ... those old red horse minnows. We were going to stay away from the cane poles and avoid blood baits.

This was the fishing trip where little-boy fishermen would become men fishermen. Whatever it took! We were going to use racket shads, purple worms, spoons, bucktails with spinners on them—but absolutely no live bait.

I remember the morning when we set out on this new adventure just like it was yesterday. I got to the marina just a little ahead of Johnson. But when I saw him drive up I thought Johnson was a little weird ... he was wearing a red bandanna. Now I told Johnson he was weird because fishing folks from Texas didn't wear rags on their heads and surely didn't wear a hat on top of that rag. Well, Johnson told me the rag was for good luck. So after I thought about it for a while I thought it was OK ... after all, I had my left pant leg rolled up a piece. Of course every fisherman from Texas knows that if the moon is full and the wind is in the east that you can catch a feast of fish if you just roll your left pant leg up a piece.

We decided we better get a start on this trip when old Johnson thought that before we did, we ought to get some minnows ... just in case. You see, he said it would be pretty tough trying to explain to the wives that we'd been fishing all day with lures and didn't catch anything. Well Johnson persuaded me, so we got us some minnows. These were big minnows. These minnows were huge. Do you know how big these minnows were? These minnows were so big that if we didn't catch any fish, we could scale and cook the minnows instead, that's how big they were.

We pushed the boat out into the water and began to paddle across the lake. It was still dark so we'd placed a gas lantern in the bow of the boat to aid us in getting to our fishing hole.

After a while we came upon what looked like a semicircle of cypress and oak trees and decided to anchor the boat. Johnson threw out the lawn mower motor. Suddenly Johnson stood up in the boat and asked me which lure I was going to use first. The boat started rocking from side to side and caused the gas lantern to tip over and fall into the water. I thought that the lantern would surely blow out when it hit the water, but to my amazement it didn't. It just sank to the bottom of the lake and gave the whole bottom of the lake this eerie glow. Johnson said something about jumping in and retrieving the lantern, but I told him not to. After all, it might act as a guiding light for the fish to come up to the boat.

Now Johnson was a good friend, but Johnson was a klutz. No sooner than we'd gotten through the lantern fiasco, Johnson said he thought he should put fresh water on the minnows. As he was picking up the minnow bucket it caught on the side of the boat and over the side went the minnows. They all swam right down to where the lantern was, just like it was a fire and gathered around it. I thought that this trip was surely turning into a dog day's fishing trip.

About that time the sun started to come up. The light shone through the trees. The birds began chirping and frogs began croaking. I looked over to one of the oak trees and saw a squirrel about midway up its trunk. The squirrel scampered down the tree and came over to where the trees roots tucked themselves into the water's edge. He spotted an acorn there and reached over to pick up the acorn when all of a sudden the water around the tree roots began to boil. Huge bubbles rose to the surface ... steam spewed from the water ... and suddenly a huge black bass leaped from the water, did a complete 360-degree turn, chomped up the squirrel in one bite, re-entered the water, and swam away.

Johnson looked at me, and I looked at him. We heard a sound and looked in the direction it was coming from and saw water boiling again but not as badly this time as it had before. We saw a V-shape in the water head straight for the tree roots again. Suddenly the head of this giant fish came out of the water. He spit the acorn back near the tree roots and swam away.

Johnson looked at me calmly and said, "You ought to use a lure that looks like a squirrel." Well, I didn't have a lure that looked like a squirrel, so I used my second best: I got my Bug Eyed Bucktail Water Monster. The thing was so heavy that it bent the tip of my rod halfway over. I reared back to cast it across to where the tree's roots were. It scraped the seat in the boat and hooked the bandanna Johnson had been wearing. He'd taken it off to wipe water from his face when he dumped the minnows overboard. The Bug Eyed Bucktail Water Monster and the bandanna all came to rest right where the acorn was.

I waited a second or two and then I twitched the line … the water began to boil … huge bubbles rose to the surface and steam was released. Suddenly the bottom of the lake just exploded, and a gigantic fish leaped out of the water and grabbed that Bug Eyed Bucktail Water Monster. He dove to the bottom of the lake … I hung on … he went to the left … I hung on … he went to the right … I hung on. I hung on for what seemed like hours.

Finally, I wrestled the fish up the side of the boat. This was a big fish … this was a *huge* fish. Do you know how big this fish was? This fish was so big that you could holler in his mouth and get an echo back. That's how big he was. This fish looked like he could drink whiskey with the best of them, chew tobacco, whittle and spit—and he was wearing that red bandanna around his head. I looked down at the gold hook attached to the Bug Eyed Bucktail Water Monster and I knew I couldn't hold on much longer … that hook was just straining. I hollered to Johnson, "Johnson, get the net!"

Johnson said, "I don't need a net to get that bandanna-wearing fish. I'll just get it with my hands."

When he reached and grabbed the line it gave slack and I saw a world-record fish shake his head and leap from the water. That fish jumped nineteen feet in the air. I knew it was a big fish … because when his body left the water the boat sank to the bottom of the dry lake.

I was destroyed, but Johnson still had the presence of mind to reach in and grab the lantern and put it back in the boat. He scooped up all the minnows and put them back in the minnow bucket. When that fish re-entered the water, a tidal wave slammed into the side of the boat and pushed us up on dry land. Now I know you think I'm lying, but I found the bandanna on the road sign leading out of the marina that day … it still had a scale or two on it.

MICKEY HUFFSTUTLER

ZINITA PARSONS FOWLER was a teacher and librarian for thirty-eight years before she began her career as an accomplished author and storyteller. She was a featured teller at the first-ever Texas Storytelling Festival in 1986 and has served on the board of the Tejas Storytelling Association. She has published numerous books, including *Ghost Stories of Old Texas* and her current release, *Gotcha!* Her recent novel, *The Last Innocent Summer,* was optioned by Sissy Spacek for an upcoming motion picture and was named Best Book of the Year by the Texas Institute of Letters.

Pretzel-Faced Willie

ZINITA PARSONS FOWLER

People of my generation will recognize this as being adapted from the old African folktale "Epaminondas." Still others will know the Appalachian version, "Lazy Jack." Indeed, variants appear in the folklore of Japan, Ireland, Portugal, and Germany, and many other cultures. This is a story my mother used to tell the family all the time—it was always a favorite. I enjoy telling it to kids because they begin to see what is going to happen—it's a story full of positive reactions.

Once on a time, in the deep piney woods of East Texas, there lived a little boy named William Brown with his mama and his papa. Down the road a piece and 'round the bend was a small brown house where his grandma lived. She loved William more that anything. Fact is, almost every time William went to see her— that was just about every day—she gave him something to take home with him.

William was a good boy and tried his best to mind his mama and his papa and his grandma. Trouble was, William wondered a lot about things like trees and horses and clouds. And when William got to wondering, he twisted his face all up funny, this way and that from wondering so hard, and he didn't listen to what he was being told.

William's face looked so funny all twisted up out of shape when he got to wondering that his Uncle Bill took to calling him Pretzel-Faced Willie. And the name stuck.

One day, early in the morning, William decided to go see his grandma. So he went down the road apiece and 'round the bend and up to the small house where she lived. The minute he stepped up on the porch, he smelled something all sweet and spicy in the air. Gingerbread! His grandma was cooking gingerbread!

Just as William went into the kitchen, she was taking a pan of gingerbread out of the oven. She set William down at the kitchen table and gave him a big piece of hot gingerbread to eat, all dripping with melted butter. And then he went out into the back yard to play with Old Belle, the hound dog, and her litter of pups.

When it was time for him to go home, his grandma cut off a big square of the fresh-cooked gingerbread and said, "Now, Willie, I want you to take this gingerbread home to your mama and papa for supper. You take care how you hold it tight in your hands so it won't drop in the dirt."

It just happened that Willie was watching a big old red dirt-dauber that had come in from the outside with him. It was crawling up and down the window screen looking for a place to get out. Willie was wondering how long it would take him to find the hole in the screen that was just big enough for a dirt-dauber to squeeze through, and he had his face all twisted up, this way and that.

"Pretzel-Faced Willie!" his grandma said, louder now because she saw he was wondering. "Did you hear me?"

"Yes'm, Grandma. I heard you."

William took the big piece of gingerbread in his hands and started up the road toward home. He was holding it ever so careful because he sort of remembered his grandma telling him not to drop it in the dirt. The closer he got to home, the tighter he clenched his fingers around the gingerbread, because he was a good boy and wanted to mind his grandma.

His mama was out in the side yard, pulling Johnson grass out of her zinnia patch. She saw William coming down the road with his hands all clenched tight in front of him.

"Willie, what do you have in your hands?" she called.

William unclenched his hands and held them out to show his mama. "Gingerbread, Mama," he said. "Grandma just baked it fresh today."

William's mama stared at the gooey mess. "Sakes alive, Willie Brown!" she cried. "That don't look like any gingerbread I ever saw! Now you just march straight over to the pump and wash all that stuff off your hands and then you come back over here and I'll tell you how to bring home ginger-bread when your grandma gives you some."

William went over and washed his hands and started back to his mama, drying them off on his jeans. He just happened to glance down and saw a twig on the ground with a bright green and yellow caterpillar crawling on it. He picked it up and took it with him.

"Now, Willie," his mama said, "next time your grandma gives you fresh gingerbread to bring home, this is what you do. You ask her for a nice paper napkin to wrap it in, and then you put it up under your straw hat so's you won't squench it up in your hands, and then you hurry home as fast as you can."

William had his eyes fixed on the bright green and yellow caterpillar crawling on the twig. His face was all twisted up this way and that, wondering how in the world a wiggly old worm with all those legs could turn into a big beautiful butterfly, floating out over the pasture as light as the breeze.

"Pretzel-Faced Willie!" his mama said, louder because she saw he was wondering again. "Did you hear what I said?"

"Yes'm, Mama. I heard you."

A day or so later, William decided to go and see his grandma. So he went down the road apiece and 'round the bend and up to the small brown house where she lived. He no sooner stepped up on the porch than he heard the *kerplunkety kerplunkety* sound of his grandma churning sour cream into butter in the kitchen.

Just as he walked in, the butter was ready to take out of the churn. His grandma set him down at the kitchen table and gave him a big piece of hot cornbread with the fresh churned butter melted all over it. And then he went out into the back yard to play with Old Belle, the hound dog, and her litter of pups.

When it was time for him to go home, William's grandma brought out a nice square of fresh-churned butter and said, "Willie, I want you to take this butter home to your mama and papa for supper."

William thought for a minute, because he sort of remembered what his mama had told him. He asked his grandma for a nice paper napkin, and once he was out in the yard, he wrapped up the square of butter ever so careful. Then, he took off his straw hat and put the wrapped-up square of butter on top of his head. He put his hat over the butter and started off up the road toward home.

Now, it was a hot day for early spring, and pretty soon as William walked along, he felt something begin to trickle through his hair and down the side of his face. He licked out his tongue and tasted it. Butter! William walked faster, but the faster he went, the hotter he got, and the more the butter trickled through his hair and down his face.

His mama was standing out on the front porch, shading her eyes and looking down the road to see if the postman was coming. She was expecting a Sears Roebuck catalog. She took one look at William and cried out, "Willie Brown! What on earth is that all over your face?"

William swept off his straw hat. "Butter, Mama! Grandma just churned some fresh today!"

"Sakes alive, Willie Brown!" his mama said. "You go straight over there to the pump and wash all that butter out of your hair and off your face, and then you come back here and I'll tell you how to bring home fresh-churned butter when your grandma gives you some!"

So William went over to the pump and washed all the melted butter out of his hair and off his face, and started back to his mama. Across the road in the pasture, little old Dottie, the colt that had been born earlier that spring, was rolling in the dust and kicking up her tiny heels, and William watched her as he walked along.

"Now, Willie," his mama said, "next time your grandma gives you some fresh-churned butter to bring home, this is what you do. You take it outside and find some nice big magnolia leaves to wrap it in. Then, you go down to the spring and you dip it under the cold water 'til it's all nice and firm, and then you hurry home with it just as fast as you can."

William still had his eyes on little old Dottie, who was doing her best to roll all the way over in the dust. He'd heard his Uncle Bill say that any horse could do that was worth at least fifty dollars. He had his face all twisted up this way and that, wondering if that little old colt with those long, skinny legs would ever roll all the way over, and if she'd really be worth fifty dollars if she could.

"Pretzel-Faced Willie!" his mama said, louder because she saw he was wondering again. "Did you hear what I said?"

"Yes'm, Mama. I heard you."

A day or so later, Willie decided to go see his grandma. So he went down the road apiece and 'round the bend and up to the small brown house where she lived. She was waiting for him in the front yard. In her hands, she held a fat, wiggly, little old brown-spotted pup.

"Willie, your Uncle Bill says the pups is old enough to leave their mama now, and he wants you to have this one for your very own to take home with you."

William had never been so happy in his life. He took the little pup out into the back yard and played with it for a long time.

"Thank Uncle Bill for me, Grandma," he said later on when it was time to go home. Once out in the yard, he sort of remembered what his mama had told him.

He went over to the magnolia tree and got some big leaves. Then he did his best to wrap the wiggly little old brown-spotted pup in the leaves, and took him down to the spring. He dipped him under the cold water once and he dipped him under the cold water twice. The little pup began to whine and wasn't so wiggly anymore, so Willie decided he must be nice and firm. He hurried home as fast as he could go.

William's mama was flapping the dustcloth out the door and she saw him coming. "Willie, what's that you got in your hands?" she called out.

Willie held out the little dog. "Puppy dog, Mama! A little old wiggly brown-spotted pup. Uncle Bill give him to me."

"Sakes alive, Willie Brown! The little thing's soakin' wet!" William's mama took the little pup and cradled it in her arms. "Go get me a towel and a blanket and we'll dry him off and put him out in the sun, and then I'll tell you what to do when your grandma gives you a little critter to bring home."

So William went and got a towel and a blanket and he helped his mama dry off the little pup and put him out in the sun to take a nap. As he was getting the pup settled down, he noticed the old white goose heading for the stock pond out by the barn with a little row of yellow goslings following along behind. He watched them as he went back to his mama.

"Now, Willie," she said, "next time your grandma gives you a little critter to bring home, this is what you do. You find yourself a nice piece of twine string and you tie it around his middle. Then you set him down in the road and let him come along with you."

William still had his eye on the old goose and her goslings. He watched as each tiny bit of yellow fluff stepped out into the stock pond and began to swim along just as pretty as you please. He wondered how in the world those little old ducks just knew how to swim without anyone ever teaching them, and his face was all twisted up, this way and that.

"Pretzel-Faced Willie!" his mama said, louder because she saw he was wondering again. "Did you hear what I said?"

"Yes'm, Mama. I heard you."

A day or so later, William decided to go see his grandma. So he went down the road apiece and 'round the bend and up to the small brown house where she lived. She was baking bread, and he could smell it as soon as he stepped up on the porch. When it was time for him to go home, she gave him a crusty brown loaf of the bread to take home for his mama and papa to have for supper.

William took the loaf of bread in his hands and started up the road toward home. Then he stopped, because he sort of remembered what his mama had told him. He fished around in his pockets until he found a nice piece of twine he'd been saving for junebug season. He tied it around the middle of the loaf of bread. Then he set it down in the road and started for home, pulling it along in the dirt behind him.

William's mama was headed for the pickup truck with her purse over her arm when she saw him coming down the road. She stopped in her tracks and just stared.

"Willie Brown, what on earth … ?" and she purely ran out of breath.

"Bread, Mama," William said. "Grandma just baked it today."

"Willie, Willie, Willie," his mama said. She didn't seem one bit happy about the fresh-baked bread. "You take that whatever-it-is out to the barn and feed it to the pigs, and then you come back here and wait on the porch 'til I get back from the store, you hear me?"

"Yes'm, Mama. I hear you."

Willie started for the barnyard, dragging the loaf of bread behind him. His mama stopped him.

"One more thing, Willie," she said. "I just baked five green apple pies for the grange picnic tomorrow, and they're coolin' out there on the back steps." She shook her finger at Willie. "You just be mighty careful, young man, how you step in those pies. You hear me?"

For once, Willie was looking his mama straight in the eye. He heard every word she said. His face was not twisted this way and that while he wondered about trees or clouds or horses. This time he meant to do exactly what his mama said. Like I told you before, Willie was really a very good boy at heart.

After his mama drove away in the pickup, Willie fed the loaf of bread to the hogs. Then he went out to the back steps and just as careful as could be, he stepped smack in the middle of every one of those green apple pies.

After that, Willie went out to sit on the front porch and wait for his mama to come home. This was one time she was going to be very proud of him. He was sure of it!

RODGER HARRIS is a native-born Oklahoman. Educated at Oklahoma State University and the University of Central Oklahoma, he is currently employed as Oral Historian for the Oklahoma Historical Society. He regularly performs with an old-time music group, the Falderal String Band. His stories are traditional and homemade, incorporating music and any other trick he can throw in. Rodger says he's been telling stories all his life but he only recently noticed that folks were listening.

Another Bowl of Beans

RODGER HARRIS

I first heard this story in 1975. I was working at a teachers' convention in Oklahoma City. During a slow time I was approached by an old-timer who identified himself as being eighty-nine years old. We exchanged a few comments and jokes, then he told me this story. He began it with an introduction common to the Ozarks and many of the surrounding states.

One time there was a traveler who was goin' from someplace in the Cherokee Nation to Fayetteville. He had lost his way, it was late in the day, and he was near to worn out. Then he come onto a cabin in the woods.

The traveler kept his distance and called out, "Is anyone home?"

Soon the door opened and an old skinny man came out. "Where you goin', friend?"

"I was tryin' to get to Fayetteville," the traveler replied.

"Well," said the old fella, "you gotta long ways to go and it's near dark now. Why don't you spend the night here and get an early start in the morning?"

"Oh, I couldn't do that," said the traveler, "but it's a mighty kind offer."

Just then a nice-lookin' young woman came out of the cabin and stood behind the old man. "You could stay for supper," she said. "We hardly ever get visitors 'round here."

"Well," said the traveler, "I thank you for your offer, but I wouldn't want to put you out any."

"We heard enough," said the old man. "You're goin' to stay the night!"

"Besides," says the woman, "I got a big pot of beans I've been a-cookin' all day. There's more than enough."

"Beans," said the traveler. "Beans is my favorite food. Don't see how I could turn down beans. I'll stay," he said.

Well they sat down at the table, and the woman put down a big bowl of beans at all three places. She put cornbread, sliced onions, and little pickled peppers on the table, too.

The traveler took two or three spoonfuls of beans. Then he smiled respectfully at the woman and said, "These are fine beans, some of the finest I've had."

The young woman smiled back, turned her head to the side, and winked at the traveler.

The traveler continued to eat the vittles, enjoying every bite. The woman gave a second helping to the old man and to the traveler too. Soon the traveler had finished the second helping and the woman offered him more.

"Well," he said, "these are some of the finest beans I've had, but I don't believe it would be proper to have any more."

"Well, we got plenty," she said, "and I might just throw 'em out if we don't eat them."

"Maybe one more bowl if you insist," said the traveler, and he dove in with the same interest he'd shown on the first helping.

This time as he ate, he noticed the woman smilin' and winkin' at him. The traveler didn't know what to make of the woman, but he sure liked her cookin'. Before long the traveler was eatin' on his fourth bowl of beans, and by now, the young woman was smilin' and winkin' at him as well as rubbin' her foot on the shin of his leg. He was some puzzled by this but did not know how to act except to finish those beans.

Pretty soon the woman was after the traveler to eat another helpin' of beans. He told her it wouldn't be polite to eat any more, but she filled his bowl and he continued.

This time not only was the woman smilin' and winkin' at him, she was also rubbin' his leg and lickin' her lips like she'd been eatin' fat bacon. Before long the traveler was offered more beans, but he flatly refused. "Well, the beans are on the stove if you want some more," the woman said.

The old man spoke up. "It's time to turn in," he said and looked over at the traveler. "Since there's only one bed, we'll all have to sleep together."

"I'll just sleep in the barn," said the traveler.

"No," said the old fella, "there's room in here where it's warm. Traveler, you sleep on this side, I'll sleep in the middle, and my woman on the outside."

They all piled in bed and were almost asleep when an awful ruckus broke out on the henhouse. The old man grabbed his gun and went out through the woods 'til the traveler and the woman couldn't hear him anymore.

After a few moments of stillness, the woman elbowed the traveler, smiled, and said, "Now's your chance!" And he got up and ate the rest of those beans!

GARY BROWN

A frequent festival teller and workshop presenter, ROSANNA TAYLOR HERN-DON creates her stories from personal and family experiences, often using her West Texas cattle country origin as subject matter. She holds a Ph.D. in interpersonal communication and the oral performance of literature, and has a national reputation in the field of communication as a university professor, administrator, and textbook author. In 1988 she was named one of the ten outstanding college and university professors in Texas by the Minnie Stevens Piper Foundation. She is a professor at Hardin-Simmons University, where she also teaches storytelling. In 1993 she received the John Henry Faulk Award from the Tejas Storytelling Association.

Chocolate

ROSANNA TAYLOR HERNDON

I waited a long time to tell the following story—until after I read an obituary of the last person I thought could be hurt by it. Still I rarely told the story, even in casual conversation with friends. I think I finally "storied" it for an audience because it offered a way to share a small portion of the time, place, and people who shaped me and my transitional generation. My first public audience for the story was the Texas Storytelling Festival.

I am a child of the Great Depression. I grew up in a small West Texas town where there was a large Hispanic population but very few African-Americans. The few black people I knew were adults, and since it was the 1930s, I knew them only by their first names. Even a distinguished gray-haired gentleman who worked for a local department store I knew only as James.

Now occasionally some black citizen in our town was given a title of respect, usually in deference to his or her great age: the title was *Aunt* or *Uncle*. That was the case with Aunt Georgia. She was a tiny, dried-up woman who lived in a small apartment behind the big house next door.

Aunt Georgia had been born in slavery. She was "about eight years old," she guessed, at the time of the emancipation.

Next to her apartment, there was a shed, and inside there were several large trunks with padlocks on them. The older children in the neighborhood whispered to us that those trunks were full of money! But I know now that wasn't true, because Aunt Georgia was a retired schoolteacher. Any teacher can guess what she really kept in those trunks—books, letters from favorite students, and little mementos that dearly remembered children had made for her years ago. Aunt Georgia loved children. She always had time for me.

Then there was Lillian. Lillian was a warm, smiling woman who supplied all of the parenting and most of the love I knew for the first few years of my life, and because it was 1934 and I was four years old, I took for granted the fact that I called her "my Lillian," and she called me "Miss Rosy."

The world was still small to me then, a swirl of people, of comings and goings that revolved around the house on Third Street, the first place I remember as home.

Along behind the house was a wide graveled alleyway that ran for several blocks through the town. It dead-ended up the street to the west at the First Christian Church, which marked the official beginning of the business district. That alley was the scene of just about all the cultural activity I was aware of in my young life. It was a great place for the neighborhood children to play.

Now, I was the only small child in the neighborhood except for my best friend, Peppy—"Pep" for short. He lived across the street, and every afternoon he came past with his grandfather on the way up into the next block to visit his great-grandmother, who was quite ill. Sometimes he got to stop and play. But because we were only four, we were not allowed to cross the street alone, so most of the time I just tagged along behind the older children.

I was always at their heels on long summer evenings. That's when the adults sat on their front porches to watch the traffic pass, water their lawns, or just visit with neighbors, while the children in the neighborhood played hide-and-seek along the alleyway. I wasn't very good at the game. I usually hid in the same place, or I giggled and got caught. But my mother said they had to let me play.

One day into that familiar scene came a boy like no one I had ever known. I'll never forget the first time I saw him. The older girls were making mud pies in the alley behind our house. They were taking the "dough" from my mother's flower bed, patting it out thin, and cutting it into shapes with some old rusty cookie cutters. Then they peeled the pieces out and set them on a row of bricks at the edge of the alleyway to dry. Pep and I were playing nearby. We looked up to see the older boys coming down the alley from the west, and with them was a child we had never seen before. He was a boy of perhaps six or seven, tall for his age, and thin. He had enormous brown eyes, and curly, curly hair, almost as red as mine.

As they came down the alley, one of the older boys scooped up one of the mud pies and with a smirk, took the new boy firmly by the arm. He said, "Hey, you like chocolate? How about a piece of fudge?" He thrust one of the mud pies into the boy's hand.

I saw him lift it slowly toward his face. I yelled, "Hey, don't! That's ..." But about that time one of the older boys stepped in front of me, grabbed me by the shoulders, and said, "Shut up, runt! You'll ruin everything." By the time I had wiggled free and stepped out where I could see again, the boy was chewing solemnly. The bigger boy was saying, "Pretty good, isn't it? You like fudge, don't you?" The boy swallowed and nodded silently. "Here. Have another one," demanded the older boy, and shoved another mud pie into the boy's hand.

The name stuck. Everyone in the neighborhood called him "Chocolate." I never knew his real name, but Chocolate and I became great friends that summer. He had time to play with me when the older children didn't. He coached me at hide-and-seek. He was good at it! He knew all the very best places to hide and showed me how to be very, very still. He said if I could keep still enough, I would be *invisible*.

During the daytime we played in the sandpile behind my house or on the swing. Sometimes we sat on a stone bench next to the fish pond and fed stale crackers to the fish. Sitting there we listened to Aunt Georgia tell us tales about faraway places. She called it Geography. I could tell Aunt Georgia enjoyed our company.

I did notice, however, that when Chocolate was there, Lillian always seemed to be just a little bit out of sorts. Oh, she brought milk and cookies to the stone bench in the back yard, but more than once I heard her say, "Your daddy's somebody special in this town. You ought not be playing with the likes of him."

The likes of him? I only knew that Chocolate was my friend.

One late summer evening, the older children were all gone somewhere except for one big boy named Zach. Zach and I tried to play hide-and-seek, but it's just not a lot of fun if there are only two. Zach finally had a great idea. We'd go up the alley to see if Chocolate could come and play, because Chocolate was so good at hide-and-seek. As we went up the alley, I stretched my legs as far as I could, trying to match my steps to Zach's longer stride. I felt very proud to be going somewhere with an older boy who was not my brother.

As we came to the side street, I knew I was not supposed to cross, but I wasn't going to admit that to Zach. So I hesitated just a bit. Then we crossed the side street into the alley of the next block. There was a large gray Packard parked in the alleyway. We circled the Packard and found ourselves at the base of a wooden stairwell leading up to a garage apartment. I knew where we were then. We were directly behind the home of Pep's great-grandmother. Chocolate lived there with his mother, who took care of the elderly woman.

When I looked way up, I could see through a screen door into the kitchen at the top of the stairs. To the right of the door, there was a woman cooking dinner. In the center of the room a single lightbulb dangled from a cord. Under the light a man in his undershirt was seated at the kitchen table. He was reading the newspaper aloud to the woman while she cooked. As we appeared, the two of them were laughing about something he had just read. It was an ordinary scene in that neighborhood … almost.

My friend Chocolate was sitting about halfway down the stairs, holding a handful of pebbles. One by one he was dropping them through the boards of the step into the alley below. When we asked if he could play, he bounded up the steps into the kitchen, slamming the screen door behind him.

I watched as he spoke first to the woman at the stove, then turned to the man at the table. The man put down the newspaper, slipped his arm around the child and pulled him close. Laughing, he said something we couldn't hear. He ruffled the child's hair and kissed him on the forehead. Then, shaking his head with a smile, he gave the child a gentle swat on the bottom as he ran back to the screen door. Slamming the door behind him, Chocolate leaned over the rail and said something that sent my world spinning: "I can't play now. My papa says it's suppertime."

I stood in that alleyway a long time, rooted in the gravel, staring up at the picture of that kitchen framed by the screen door. I was frantically trying to phrase a question I had no words for. When I came to my senses, I realized that Zach was already around the big Packard and halfway to the cross street. I ran after him yelling, "Hey, Zach! Wait a minute, I ..." But I never did ask the question.

You see, the woman at the stove was Chocolate's pretty mother. I knew her. She was black. But the man at the kitchen table, the man in his undershirt reading the newspaper to her, was a white man. I knew him too. He didn't live in the garage apartment. Yet Chocolate had said, "My papa says it's suppertime." *My papa.* Although I often puzzled over that statement, I never mentioned it to Chocolate, just as I never mentioned the mud pies. You see, there was a question welling up inside me. I kept struggling with it, but I didn't exactly know what the question was.

Summer soon ended, and Chocolate went back to wherever he lived with his grandmother during the winter to go to school. That fall we moved away from that neighborhood, and in December Pep's great-grandmother died. I never saw Chocolate or his mother after that. Oh, once later, when I was a teenager, I thought I saw him downtown with some other boys. I started to call out to him. But by then, I knew that "Chocolate" was not an appropriate name for a boy, and I didn't know his real name. With a teenager's awkwardness, I decided not to speak.

The man I had seen sitting at the table that day was a different matter. I saw him often while I was growing up in the little town. His name was Troy Vincent. I saw him coming and going from the bank. I saw him on the street corner talking business with other men. I knew Mr. Vincent was in the oil business with his brother in Dallas, and that they owned some large tracts of ranchland. The first time I heard the term *multimillionaire,* it was in reference to Troy Vincent.

Mr. Vincent lived just two blocks from us in a large brick house with his pale, quiet wife. The Vincents weren't exactly part of the social scene in that town; they were just always *there.* They had no children. I saw Mrs. Vincent coming and going in the big gray Packard, or occasionally leaving the First Methodist Church. As a teenager I sometimes waited on her in the local department store. I never heard her speak above a whisper. She was always alone, and there seemed to be a kind of sadness about her.

Once, in my teens, I asked my father about Troy Vincent. I wanted to know what kind of man he was. My father, who was never one to criticize, said, "I don't know a thing bad about him, except that he seems to be his own worst enemy." Only after I was grown did I realize that was a phrase Dad reserved for people who had self-destructive habits—alcoholism or compulsive gambling. But about Troy Vincent, I never did know.

In time I grew up, went away to college, and never came back to live in that little town. From time to time, however, when my parents sent me letters, they included clippings of interest from the local newspaper.

One morning in Boston I pulled from my mailbox a letter fat with clippings. As I spread them out on the table in front of me I saw the lead article from the newspaper's front page. It read, TROY VINCENT MURDERED. I unfolded and read the clippings. Then I began searching for the obituary. As I read it, I saw there were listed as survivors the pale wife, the brother in Dallas, and two nephews. No children were listed. There was no mention of my friend Chocolate.

It seems Troy Vincent had been found more than half a mile from the nearest road in the middle of a pasture, stretched out on his back. He was wearing a three-piece suit and a white shirt and tie—all neatly arranged. His arms were folded ceremoniously across his chest. There was a hat pulled all the way down over his eyes and his ears. He had been shot in the abdomen at point-blank range with a shotgun. No weapon was found at the scene. There were no footprints, no clues. No one was ever apprehended for the murder.

I thought about my friend Chocolate and wondered were he was.Now, I'd like to tell you that his father sent him to Harvard School of Business, made him a partner in his oil firm, and left him a fortune. The truth of the matter is, I don't know what became of him.

But one morning, twelve or fourteen years ago, I was having breakfast with my husband, Pep Herndon—the boy from across the street. Out of the blue, he wanted to know: "How well do you remember that gang of kids on Third Street?"

"Well," I said, "I remember some of them pretty well."

He asked, "Do you remember a boy we called 'Chocolate'?"

Did I remember Chocolate! I said, "Sure, I remember him."

Next he wanted to know, "What was his name, really?"

I blurted out, "I don't know what his real name was, but it should have been Troy Vincent, Jr."

Pep stopped with his coffee cup in midair and stared at me for a long moment. When he finally set the cup down, he announced, "Well, I hope he's up to his elbows in oil wells, and he makes those old boys eat dirt."

With the Help of Sterling

ROSANNA TAYLOR HERNDON

I told this story in bits and pieces for years before I ever tried to put it together. When people talked about wild and crazy kids they knew, I sometimes told episodes about Sterling. As a former teacher of talented and gifted children, I recognized Sterling as truly exceptional. I hope you will too.

I was a young teacher of talented and gifted children when I first moved into that neighborhood. Almost immediately, the neighbors began to tell me about the escapades of a child they referred to in sarcastic tones as That Morrison Kid. I saw in him all the characteristics that my unusually bright students exhibited. His name was Sterling. When we met, he was only seven years old, and already he needed someone who was "on his side." We quickly developed a mutual admiration.

Sterling was the son of Dr. and Mrs. Morrison across the street. Dr. Morrison was head of the surgery department at the nearby medical school, and Mrs. Morrison was a quiet gentle woman who seemed to be a bit fragile. Now, she had raised two children to their teens, and there had been nothing unusual about those two. They were, in fact, rather ordinary bookish children, and *then came Sterling*. Dr. Morrison was one of those people who tries to solve all relationship problems with gifts. I think he understood the child fairly well, still he didn't give the boy much of his time. So Sterling roamed the neighborhood, to the horror of Mrs. Ballard.

Mrs. Ballard was an elderly woman who lived next door to them. She had long since forgotten what it was like to be a child. But she had a small white poodle named Penelope, and she treated Penelope like a child. She protected Penelope from everything, including her granddaughter who occasionally came to visit, but mostly she protected Penelope from That Morrison Kid.

Now, Sterling had three major interests. First, he was interested in animals. He had never owned an animal, but he liked them a lot. He was fascinated with machinery and everything that was mechanical. He had become quite skillful at taking things apart to see how they worked. Of course, he wasn't quite as good at putting them back together again. Third, and perhaps most important, Sterling wanted to know all about anatomy.

He'd seen the skeletons at the medical school. He thought they were wonderful, especially all those tiny little bones in the hands and feet. He inspected those bones from every angle, and he didn't understand his mother's aversion to the idea that they had once been part of living things. He thought that only made them more interesting. These bones were *real*.

On a short vacation they took him to the Smithsonian. He saw those gigantic mounted skeletons, and he was awed by them. He told me it was his dream to find a huge fossilized skeleton and put it together himself. Then he'd own it, he said, so he could look at it every day. His dad bought him a book about how the big skeletons were put together, and how the researchers knew which bones went where. That gift really pleased him.

So for his eighth birthday, I gave him a book, with overlay pages, about the anatomy of mammals. The basic page showed each animal's major organs. The first overlay showed its skeletal structure. The next added muscles, and the final overlay was the exterior of the mammal. I have rarely given a gift that brought so much pleasure. He thought it was the best book he'd ever seen, except perhaps for the one from the Smithsonian. He carried those books almost everywhere.

He wasn't a bad child. In fact, he was always trying to be helpful. It's just that things always seemed to turn out wrong for Sterling. You see, he didn't think the way many people expect a child to think. At least he didn't think the way *Mrs. Ballard* expected children to think.

Well, Mrs. Ballard's granddaughter came to spend a few days and brought with her a stuffed animal—a fuzzy toy poodle, bright pink. The children thought it was a lot prettier than Penelope. They named it Penny, after the real dog, and they often commented that Penelope seemed a bit pale by comparison.

One morning Sterling was watching his mother frost little cakes for a baby shower. He wasn't interested in baby showers, he knew all about babies, but he was intrigued that just two drops of red food coloring could turn a whole bowl of plain white frosting a beautiful shade of pink.

Later in the day, his mother was dressing for the party and the two children were playing in the backyard. Suddenly, Mrs. Morrison heard her neighbor, Mrs. Ballard, screaming. She ran to the back door, putting on her robe as she came. From the breezeway she thought she was seeing the child's toy poodle standing in a large pan on a picnic bench. As she got closer she could see it *wasn't* the pink toy at all. It was *Penelope!* The frightened children were standing nearby holding sponges. Both were dripping with red and pink, and Mrs. Ballard was truly hysterical.

Penelope wasn't in bad shape. Most of her head was still white. Her body was a lovely shade of pink. But then Mrs. Ballard grabbed the little poodle from the pan and clutched it to her chest, with red dye splashing down her dress and shoes. That's when you could see that where Penelope had been standing in the solution, her feet and legs were a beautiful, deep, cherry red. As Sterling backed away from Mrs. Ballard, he was saying, "We were just trying to help."

Later, Sterling's account of that episode was rather different from Mrs. Ballard's: he said the problem really was that Mrs. Ballard had come too soon, and they hadn't finished. If she had come later, she'd have seen that Penelope could look as pretty as the stuffed poodle. He also confided to me that they had run out of the red food coloring because they added too much water. Needing a darker color, they had made a trip to the Mom and Pop grocery around the corner, and had bought some Rit, a fabric dye, and that's what really did the job.

The veterinarian's bill for making Penelope white again was rather large. Dr. Morrison paid it—but he wasn't happy, and Mrs. Ballard never let Sterling anywhere near that little dog again. In fact, the sight of him riding his bike at the end of the block always caused her to grab the little poodle and run for the house. In the neighborhood now, people rarely said Sterling's name. They called him The Kid Who Painted the Poodle Pink.

Sterling was really sad that Mrs. Ballard didn't like him, and he vowed to do something to make amends. So, one day when he heard the granddaughter say, "My grandmother caught a mouse in the kitchen this morning," he wanted to know: "What did she *do* with the mouse?" The child said, "I don't know. I guess she put it in the trash can in the alley."

Late that afternoon, Sterling's mother saw him digging in a flower bed. When she asked what he was doing, he answered with his usual straightforwardness that he was "burying a dead mouse." His mother thought, "Isn't that sweet? Maybe there's hope for Sterling yet." She soon forgot the mouse. She had begun to forget a lot of things.

Sterling's mother was becoming distant. She talked vaguely of when the older children were young. Her family and friends were beginning to be concerned about her ability to cope. She cried a lot, but Dr. Morrison insisted she should just "Snap out of it: a lot of people have young children at our age." Besides, he said, Sterling was "just being a boy."

The Morrisons' teenagers had become a bit worried about their mother's mental health, and during spring break they tried to help. They kept Sterling busy all week long by building a treehouse, and Sterling thought it was a grand place to play. No one noticed him digging in the flower bed from time to time, and things were quiet in the neighborhood ... until summer came.

The older children both had summer jobs, and Sterling began to spend most of every day in the treehouse. I sometimes saw him climbing the ladder to the treehouse with one of those favorite books clamped tightly under his arm. He confided to me that he was making a gift for Mrs. Ballard.

Finally one day he appeared at my house to show off the completed gift. I was impressed by the eight-year-old's patience and accomplishment. I was even more impressed with his understanding of gift-giving. But I must admit, I watched apprehensively as he rang Mrs. Ballard's doorbell. Sterling stood on her porch beaming with pride. He held in front of him a small board left over from the treehouse. On it he had carefully mounted all the tiny delicate bones from Mrs. Ballard's very own mouse. You know, *she* didn't think it was wonderful.

I think that was the week Mrs. Ballard announced her decision to move to an apartment near her daughter's family. And a neighbor up the street began referring to Sterling as The Boy Who Mounted the Mouse.

Almost immediately a new neighbor moved into the Ballard house. The Morrisons were a little worried about Sterling's relationship with the new neighbor. But this man didn't have a poodle. He didn't have a dog at all. He did have some well-built coops along his back fence where, he told us proudly, he raised prizewinning, feather-legged bantam poultry.

Now, these were the first bantam chicks Sterling had ever encountered, and he thought that little rooster was the prettiest thing he'd ever seen. That rooster was so black he glistened in the sun. He had a long elegant tail, and his little legs were thickly feathered—soft and delicate, just like fur. The hens he thought were not quite so interesting. In fact, Sterling said they looked sort of dusty, like they needed a bath. His parents told him: "Stay away from those coops!"

It was about the same time that Dr. Morrison finally began to worry about his wife's mental state. By now she was more than a little vague. She never smiled. She rarely left the house, and she was afraid to take her eyes off Sterling. She no longer let him play outdoors. Sterling began to complain there was nothing to do and that everyone had a job except him.

One morning Dr. Morrison said, "Sterling, I've decided that you can go to work with me for a while. I'll hire you. I'll pay you ten cents an hour to run errands. We'll have a grand time." Sterling was ecstatic because he was finally leaving the ranks of the unemployed. Mrs. Morrison agreed to the plan, but she made her husband promise to keep the boy away from gruesome things—the morgue, the specimen room, and the anatomy lab.

The first day went pretty well. He ran errands for the whole department. He went for coffee; he went for Cokes. He had lunch with his dad in the cafeteria, sitting at the table with the two medical students who worked for his dad during the summer. He felt very important.

By the end of the second afternoon, however, he was running out of errands and was farmed out to the departmental secretary. He quickly mastered the filing system. He sharpened pencils, stuffed envelopes, carried messages, and collected the mail. Eventually he was down to sorting paper clips, and the secretary was beginning to look weary.

The third morning the secretary called in sick, and Sterling was donated to the two medical students as an assistant. They inventoried surgical instruments. They sharpened instruments. They prepared surgical packs. Sterling wanted to know the name of *everything*. He was fascinated with the big sterilizer and the autoclave. During the 185 questions he asked every hour, he discovered the two medical students were making *four dollars an hour*. He didn't think that stacked up very well against his dime.

At noon in the cafeteria line he tried to talk to his dad about the inequity of his pay. His dad said, "Oh, Sterling, don't be ridiculous," as he reached for a slice of lemon pie. On the way home he brought up the subject again saying, "If they're worth four dollars an hour, I should be worth at least two dollars an hour, don't you think?" His father barely heard him because he was watching traffic and worrying about how his wife's day had gone. He said, "Sterling, I don't want to hear any more about this."

Now you must remember, *Sterling tried to negotiate.*

On Thursday the secretary was still "sick." In fact, after inquiring about Sterling, she mentioned the possibility of taking the rest of her available leave time.

Dr. Morrison tried to keep the boy busy. He sent him on all kinds of errands—to the mailroom, for Cokes, and to carry messages here and there. By about the middle of the afternoon, Dr. Morrison had forgotten about Sterling and was busy at his desk when he heard laughter coming from the hallway. As he stepped out into the hall, he saw a crowd of his medical school colleagues and personnel from the hospital gathered along the walls of the hallway, and down the corridor marched Sterling. He was carrying a placard. The front of it proclaimed: MORRISON UNFAIR TO SON. The back of the placard read, ON STRIKE FOR $1 AN HOUR.

Dr. Morrison's face turned purple. He grabbed the boy by the shoulder, jerked him into his office, and slammed the door. Now, I don't know what was said, but they *settled* for fifty cents an hour, and of course, Sterling had finally captured his father's attention.

Friday morning, Dr. Morrison arrived for work with Sterling in tow, determined to keep him truly busy. As they passed one office, Dr. Morrison heard someone refer to Sterling as That Kid Who Went on Strike. He winced.

During the day Dr. Morrison sent Sterling on a dozen errands, but by now Sterling knew his way around the building, and almost before Dr. Morrison could get back to his own work, here Sterling would be again saying, "What can I do *now*?" In exasperation he grabbed a stack of books, pushed them across the desk to the boy and said, "Here—take these back to Dr. Greene in Anatomy." At last he could work without interruption.

93

When he finally realized he hadn't seen the child for some time, he began a mental roll-call of places he had gone to deliver messages. Suddenly, he realized he had sent him to return books to the office next to the anatomy lab. He had *promised* to keep him away from that part of the building.

He raced down the hall and met Sterling returning. He wore a grin from ear to ear. Beaming, he said, "Dad, I met this *neat* man named *Scotty.* He runs *the anatomy lab!"*

Dr. Morrison's heart sank.

Sterling continued excitedly, "Let me tell ya, he let me help him straighten cadavers and put on covers! You know, Scotty has this pulley system, and you can pull the cadavers up on one side of the room, and swing them across and let them down on the other side."

Dr. Morrison wasn't listening. He was thinking, *His mother's going to kill me.*

It was, in fact, the last day that Sterling went to work with his father, but he'd had a great week. His mother had a rest, and Dr. Morrison had gained a new appreciation for his wife's dilemma and her vagueness. He decided to do something nice for her.

On Saturday afternoon, he went shopping, because he knew something she really wanted. It was the newest of the newfangled gadgets for house-wives—an automatic washing machine. It was made by the Bendix Corpo-ration. This front-loading washer operated much like the present-day drier. It had a round glass door in the front, a little like a porthole, and if you watched while it ran, you could see the suds and the clothes go floating past the glass door as the tumbler rotated.

Now, the Bendix washers had one major disadvantage. They vibrated. They vibrated so badly they had to be bolted to the floor—preferably to a concrete slab. The Morrisons put theirs on the breezeway at the back of the house. Sterling watched from the house while it tumbled the clothes over and over. What a marvelous invention! He waited a few days before he begged to load it himself. His mother finally said, "All right, but don't put in anything except your own playclothes."

It really went pretty well, except for the bubble gum he had left in the pocket of a shirt, and the small garden toad he had carefully tucked into the pocket of a pair of jeans … He didn't quite understand why a bath would kill a garden toad.

The next Saturday, Dr. Morrison decided he would take his wife out for the afternoon, just the two of them. He hired the two teenagers, who had the day off, to watch Sterling. The afternoon went smoothly until the older boy went out on the front porch to visit with a friend, and his sister's boyfriend called on the telephone. By the time their parents returned, the scene had changed.

The Morrisons had had a pleasant time. Mrs. Morrison had perked up a little before the afternoon was over and even laughed several times, but … as they turned into the driveway they were met by the new neighbor. He was shouting something about a threat to sue. Dr. Morrison ran up the driveway, around to the back of the house, where already a small crowd of neighbors had gathered.

Sterling was backed up against the wall of the house. He was shaking from head to toe, and he was in tears. The Bendix was running. As Dr. Morrison approached, he couldn't believe his eyes! The machine was vibrating wildly and there were strange sounds coming through the glass door. Along with the suds you could see what appeared to be feathers. He grabbed the handle forcing the safety latch, and the door swung open. Out poured water, suds, and two wet bedraggled Bantam hens. Most of their feathers were gone. The few that were left were wet, and mostly broken. The hens made horrible little sounds as they staggered dizzily across the breezeway, holding their heads at rather peculiar angles. Dr. Morrison was beside himself. He shouted at the frightened child, "What's wrong with you? You're the strangest kid I ever saw." Then he was horrified at his own loss of control. Sterling cried harder and tried to say, "I was just trying to help."

Dr. Morrison wrote the neighbor a check for the "damages."

He'd have written one for almost any amount to placate the angry man. The following week was unpleasant at the Morrisons' house.

A week or two later, Dr. Morrison wanted to take his wife for a Sunday afternoon drive, but leaving Sterling was out of the question. They put him in the back seat of the car. Somewhere on the outskirts of town, a small voice from the backseat said, "See that billboard?" They looked up to see a frequently seen advertisement for the *New Bendix*. The round door was open, and looking out through the door was a small furry kitten. Approaching from the left was a mother cat, carrying another kitten in her mouth. The caption, unfortunately, said: *Safe Enough for Your Softest Treasures.* From the back seat of the car Sterling continued. "See, if it's all right for kittens, why doesn't it work for frogs and chickens?"

After that, no one in the neighborhood ever said the Morrison child's name again. He was always referred to as The Kid Who Put the Chickens in the Bendix. Except for me. I always called him Sterling, because Sterling is a precious commodity with the potential for becoming a wonderful work of art.

MERRYL HARTMAN

AYUBU KAMAU was born in Oklahoma and migrated to Texas a few years back. An exceptional storyteller who blends music with the stories of his African and American ancestry, he is one of only five tellers to ever perform three times at the Texas Storytelling Festival. He has performed at schools and festivals across the nation, including the National Festival of Black Storytelling. He lives in Dallas, where he is a regular performer at the city's Martin Luther King Center.

An Old Nigerian Tale

AYUBU KAMAU

This moralizing tale came to me while I traveled to cities and towns throughout Oklahoma. There is a more literal version in which an actual cow's tongue is presented to the OBA. I chose to adapt the story to speak to man's higher self.

OBA, a chief in Yoruba society, wanted to know of the most positive of all things given to man by God Obatala. A servant was sent out to find this positive thing and return it to the OBA.

The servant went out to seek the positive thing. He climbed to the top of the highest mountain in the land. He thought, meditated, and thought; then he talked to the animals who lived nearby, to the women who gathered their roots and berries in the bush lands. He spoke to the men who hunted for game with crude metal spears.

Then, on the wings of a giant hawk, the servant flew to the OBA's house with the news that the most positive thing given to man is the tongue!

"The tongue!"

"Yes, the tongue. With the tongue we create friendships that last a lifetime, lovers' hearts are made to be as one, for always.

"With the tongue, wisdom is passed from one mind to the next and one generation to the next making for friends and wise counsel. Peace is created between nations so the young don't go off to die.

"The most positive thing in the world," said the servant, "is the tongue!"

Then OBA, a chief in Yoruba society, wanted to know the most negative thing given to man by God Obatala.

The servant went out to seek the negative thing. He sailed in a boat down the River Niger to the sea. He sat on the rocks and watched the waves go out and flow in to crash upon the shore. Out and in … out and in. He thought, meditated, and thought; he talked to the fish of the water, to the animals who walked along the shore. He spoke with the women who washed their clothes on the rocks. He talked to the men who pulled their harvest from the sea.

Then, on the back of a friendly crocodile, the servant rode to the OBA's house with the news that the most negative thing given to man is … the tongue!

"The tongue!"

"Yes, the tongue. With the tongue we tell lies and spread the gossip that breaks friendships apart and leaves lovers' hearts broken, sometimes for all time.

"With the tongue, ignorance is encouraged, and hatred is spread among us, making us enemies instead of friends. We give bad counsel, create wars among nations, and send the young off to die, leaving the elders at home to cry.

"The most negative thing in the world," said the servant, "is the tongue!"

"How are they at once the most positive and the most negative?" asked the OBA.

"Obatala," said the servant, "has given us the tongue, and a mind that gives it the messages it takes to the world."

SHREVEPORT TIMES

HARRIET LEWIS has worked since 1983 with the Shreveport Regional Arts Council's Artist-in-Education program and is currently a Visiting Artist touring four parishes in northwest Louisiana. She is listed as a performing artist on the Louisiana Division of Arts' Artist Roster. Harriet was featured as a regional teller at the 1992 National Storytelling Conference and as a guest teller at the 1994 Texas Storytelling Festival. She is a graduate of Louisiana Tech University and Washburn University, Kansas. She lives in Benton, Louisiana, off Linton Road in back of a field, just behind pear trees.

Aunt Tucky

HARRIET LEWIS

I could always trust Evie to tell the truth. Evie was old—maybe fifty. She was a deaconess in her church; she absolutely would not tell a lie. I was ten and a half and knew lots of stuff. The subject of witches opened while we were shelling peas. I, the star of the Summer Reading Program, stated, "There's no such thing as witches that do magic ... Subject closed."

It was until Evie quietly responded, "But I know what I know ..." Subject open again. Evie continued shelling peas and began remembering out loud to me. I kept shelling peas and listened:

Back when I was a girl, there was a woman lived way back on the Cypress Bayou, away from everybody else. She had a shabby little cabin. To the front, she had two plank boards for steps and a rough board door. Across the back, there was a porch built out over the edge of the bayou. She was a couple of miles above us on the right fork of Linton Road and about a quarter-mile down the first dirt trail to the right. She was a witch-woman; everybody said so.

She had a bunch of children out at the little place—which was passing strange since she wasn't married. We thought maybe she stole them. Anyhow, she would never let them around other people, church, school, or nothing. She just kept them out there working them, and teaching them witch-woman ways.

We all knew that if a man had a fight with someone, all he had to do was walk down that dirt path to Aunt Tucky's place—that's her name, Aunt Tucky. He could walk up those two wooden steps, rap on the board door and call out, "Aunt Tucky, Aunt Tucky!" The door would crack open. The old woman would peer out and snap. "What you want?"

That man could tell her how he was mad at whoever. He could say, "I want you to give him a whammy. Put a bad spell on him!"

And from behind the door, Aunt Tucky would say, "Cross my palm with money." One bony hand would stretch out, palm up, fingers waiting. (It did not take much. Two bits would do.)

When that quarter was placed in Tucky's hand, she pulled it in. Still behind the door, she'd say, "Name the man." After the name was named, business was done. That man on the doorstep could go on home.

Within five days, guaranteed, something would happen to the one named. It could be that the man would be cutting firewood to sell for Christmas money. He could be cutting with a brand new axe or a trusty old one. Didn't matter. His axe was going to break! Old or new, it would break. And he'd have to spend all his money on a new one! Bad luck! Or, that man's best, favorite coon-hunting dog—perfectly strong and healthy—would be turning around to take a nap. That dog would fall over, *blap!* Dead on the ground! A friend gone and lots less meat on the table 'til he's replaced. Bad luck from Aunt Tucky! Or one of the feller's children—run those fields, climb those trees, swim that bayou—one of them would fall off his own back porch. The child would break all four legs! Yes! Four legs. I said that to show you *double* bad luck! That man would have to take off work, take the child to the doctor. See, he lost money from his work, and lost money on the doctor. Double bad luck from Aunt Tucky the witch-woman.

We all knew about hexes and spells, but some people claimed there was more. Some heard that at the moment the sun set and the night breeze began, Aunt Tucky could shed her skin. She could slip out of her skin and become like a spirit or a ghost or a haunt. The children whispered that Tucky could catch the night wind and ride it across the bayou waters, sifting herself through the moss and stirring the foggy, black water. Going who-knows-where and doin' who-knows-what! All night, until the dawn. Then she'd ride the wind across her back porch and call, "Skin, my skin. Let me in." Tucky would slide back into her skin. She'd walk back into the house just as if she'd been on God's green earth all along. That is what she'd do back in those woods, and nobody around to see!

One summer evening, Tucky called her children together and told them she was going away. "You big ones take care of the little ones," she said. "Sit by the fireplace, keep the front door locked. If anybody comes knocking on the door and calling 'Aunt Tucky,' don't open the door. Just answer them and say, 'Ain't no Aunt Tucky here!' They will think they got the wrong place and go away. Stay here, sit still. Watch for me and wait. I'll be back."

Then she called one of the big children to come to the back porch with her. Aunt Tucky told the child to pick up the skin when Tucky shed it. Most important, the child had to hang the skin on the nail on the wall next to the porch ... That was so Aunt Tucky could get back in it easy.

Tucky began to moan, "Skin, my skin ... Let it begin." She simmered; she glowed. Her old brown skin slid down to the porch floor. Aunt Tucky was like a spirit or a haunt! Floating up and out, lighter than a spider's silk thread, she hitched to the night wind and rode away across the dark bayou waters.

The poor child did what she was told. So Aunt Tucky's skin, all wrinkled up, was hung on the nail on the back porch wall: and the children sat inside by the fireplace waiting. But Aunt Tucky did not come back the next morning. They all got hungry; the little ones cried. Still the big ones made them stay put because Tucky had told them to stay. They's scared of her. So, they waited through another day and night. The big ones were so hungry they wanted to cry, too.

When the sun rose proud-high, on the third day, the big ones took the little ones by the hand saying, "Come on! We're going somewhere where people take care of their children—where people care about being with their families." They walked out that wooden front door, down those two plank steps, to the road, and to the first neighbor's house they could find. Before those children could finish telling her about being hungry and Aunt Tucky being gone, that good neighbor-woman was already cooking. She filled those empty stomachs with biscuits and white gravy 'til they were full satisfied. Then she told them to go back to their cabin place. Aunt Tucky would be looking for them if she had come back, you see. "But I'll come check on you before the day is over," she promised. So they went back to sit still, and watch and wait.

The neighbor lady took some of her egg money, caught a ride to town and bought a ham and a big bag of salt. How she got all that out to Aunt Tucky's before dark, I don't know. But she did. Late in the day, the neighbor-lady came down the path. She called to the children—not knocking—so they let her in. Seeing that Tucky hadn't come back, she fried them some ham. They ate, then sat by the fireplace again, watching the neighbor-lady in Aunt Tucky's house. She told the big ones that she wanted to show them how to use the salt to cure ham. That could wait 'til tomorrow though. She needed to start home before dark.

"But," she said, "we've got to do something about this salt before I go. It would be rock hard if that damp air off the bayou gets to it over night!"

She began looking for a bucket with a lid, a jar or canister with a top. But she couldn't find anything. She went to the back porch. She looked up the porch—nothing. She looked down the porch—nothing. Bare, clean empty, nothing! When she turned to go back into the house, the woman spotted something hanging on the wall by the door. The children heard her say, "Here! This old hide-y-side-y thing will do!" And she lifted Aunt Tucky's skin from the nail on the wall.

The little children were scared. What should they do? What should they say? The big ones decided they should do exactly what Aunt Tucky told them. They did not say one word. They just sat still and watched and waited. They kept quiet and watched out the back door as the neighbor lady shook out the skin. She opened it wide at the top and began to scoop salt into it. They watched the lady fill the brown hidey-skin bag with the white salt, then take off a shoelace to tie tight 'round the neck of it. They kept quiet as she leaned the salt-filled skin against the back porch wall, brushed off her hands, and came back inside. She told them the sun was going down and she had to go. She'd be back tomorrow, and she told them to lock the doors after she left.

Doors locked, the children waited quietly. It was that night that Aunt Tucky returned from wandering the bayou. Her voice moved across the porch calling, "Skin, my skin … Let me in."

But something was wrong! The salt! The salt poured into Aunt Tucky's skin had dried and shrunk the skin! The hide was shriveled so that Aunt Tucky could not fit. Also, the knot of shoelace at the throat top was pulled tight. Being a spirit-thing, Tucky couldn't force the knot undone! Aunt Tucky forced the breeze across the porch again; her voice was anxious.

"Skin, skin, always lucky. Welcome home your Aunt Tucky."

Nothing happened.

Again and again they heard her beg, "Skin, my skin. Let me in."

But she could not get in.

Tucky whipped up a fury wind and began to howl and moan. She rode the wind full force, battered the front door—*blam! blam! blam!*—calling "It's Aunt Tucky-y-y, it's Aunt Tucky!" But the children had been told what to do when someone knocked against the door. They huddled close, and shouted, "Ain't no Aunt Tucky! No Tucky here. No Tucky here. Go away!"

Tucky went some kind of mad! She started trying to tear down the house. She'd make those children help her get back her skin. She whipped the wind 'round the house, rattled the cracked windows, shook walls. She pulled shingles from the roof. Those poor children sat waiting and watching. Tucky and the wind seemed to be shaking the house apart.

Through the night Aunt Tucky's voice called "Skin, my skin. Let me in-n-n. It's-s-s Aunt Tucky … y!" Through the same night, the big ones and the little ones held each other close waiting and waiting and hoping.

Their hope came through the east window. They saw the sky lighten to gray, then the earth edged with pink. Tucky's voice seemed to fade; the wind slowly went away. A beautiful golden ray of sunlight reached up from the east and glorified the cloudless morning! The night wind began to weaken. The night air had to go back to the foggy bayou and its shadow places. And Aunt Tucky had to ride away with it.

Soon as there was light enough, the big ones took the little ones by the hand and explained, "Aunt Tucky ain't never coming back. We're going to find a place where people care about their children, where people come home to their families. And we'll stay there." So they went out and down the Linton Road where they found good people. Several families took those children in and cared for them. Raised them.

Even today, people can go up Linton Road and out on that dirt path to the little cabin. It's still there and in fair shape. Nobody lives there though. I hear that if a person can walk out on the porch just at sunset, the evening breeze will begin to stir from across the bayou as dark comes. I've heard some say that on that porch just at dark ... if they are very still, and will watch and wait, they'll see the moss move. They can feel the night wind, and they can still hear a thin old voice saying, "Skin, my skin. Let me in ..." That witch-woman can't come back and she can't leave here, either. To this day, it's still Aunt Tucky.

That's what Evie told me about witches. And Evie would not tell a lie. I know what I know. Subject closed.

BARBARA McBRIDE-SMITH discovered her voice as a storyteller at the first Texas Storytelling Festival in 1986. "My name wasn't chosen for the tale tradin' that day," she remembers, "but a dear friend gave me her spot in the olio." The following year, Barbara was a featured teller at the Texas Festival, and in the years since, she has headlined at festivals and conferences across the U.S. At the same time, she has continued her career as a school library media specialist in Stillwater, Oklahoma, where she lives with her husband, a teenage son, and a golden retriever.

Pandora

BARBARA McBRIDE-SMITH

Pandora has gotten a bad rap for thousands of years. She has been blamed for every evil that plagues our lives. Why is that? It's because her story has been recorded by people with names like Hesiod, Homer, Euripides, Aristophanes. Men. It seems to me that if you hear about her from a woman's point of view, you'll get a different picture. The fact is, Pandora was framed.

Have you ever been making up your bed or fluffing up your pillow, and you come across one of those little tags that reads: UNDER PENALTY OF LAW—DO NOT REMOVE? And you think to yourself, "Who says? This is my pillow. I can rip this sucker off right now. Is the FBI gonna come in here and arrest me if I do?"

Well, that must have been how Pandora felt about that box. The box had been a wedding present from Papa Zeus. It was a beautiful box, covered with gold and inlaid with jewels. It had a heavy lid held shut by a lock. And underneath that lock there was a tag. It read: UNDER PENALTY OF LAW—DO NOT REMOVE. And Pandora probably said to herself, "Who says? This is *my* box. Papa Zeus gave it me. Why wouldn't he want me to look inside it?"

You see, Pandora had a problem.

It had all started years and years ago as a feud between Papa Zeus and the Metheus brothers. You remember the Metheus brothers. There was Pro … Prometheus. He was the oldest and the smartest. And then there was Epi … Epimetheus. He wasn't too bright, but he was real proud of his big brother. He used to say, "This here's my bro Pro. He's the brains of the family."

The Metheus boys were Titans, but they lived right alongside the mortals. They were fond of mortals and liked to give them presents. One day Pro decided to give the mortals some fire so they could warm their feet and eat cooked meat. The problem was, the only fire that existed was in Papa Zeus's barbecue pit up on Mount Olympus. So one evening while Zeus was out on an affair of state, Pro slipped in the back gate and stole a red hot coal from the fire pit. He took it down and gave it to the mortals. Well sir, that made Pro a hero with the mortals, but it chapped old Zeus's hide.

And what did Papa Zeus do about it? He punished Prometheus by hanging him on the side of a mountain. Pro hung there all day long in the boiling hot sun. And he hung there all night in the cold. Then in the wee hours of the morning an eagle flew up there, sat down on Pro's face, and started to peck at his belly. She pecked and pecked until she plucked his liver plumb out. She swallowed it and took off. Poor old Pro had to hang there again all day long in the boiling hot sun and all night long in the cold. He was miserable, shivering … liverless. But he didn't die—he couldn't die because he was immortal. So that night he grew a brand new liver. And the next morning, the eagle was back. Well, that same old routine went on day after day, month after month, year after year! The eagle thought she had a standing invitation for breakfast!

Even after eons of time had gone by, Papa Zeus still wasn't satisfied that the Metheus brothers and their pals, the mortals, had gotten their fair share of punishment for stealing his fire. So, that was when Zeus hit upon the idea of making a *woman*. That's right … the first woman! Up until then the whole world was inhabited by nothing but good old boys. Not a woman amongst them. How their toilet paper rolls ever got changed is a mystery to me.

Zeus went to his son Festus, the blacksmith, and asked him to design a creature that would drive the good old boys crazy. What Festus built was a woman. He made her strong and he made her beautiful. Zeus made her smart .. *and* he made her curious. Then Zeus named her Pandora, which means "gift to all."

You getting my drift here? It was a setup right from the start! Papa Zeus gave Pandora that beautiful box (the one covered with gold and inlaid with jewels), and he sent her off to find Epimetheus and marry up with him. The moment Epi laid eyes on Pandora, he was in love. So they got married. She promised to love, honor, and redecorate. And she got busy straightening out the sock drawer of his life.

For the first couple of weeks, Pandora was working so hard at being domestic she didn't think much about that box. But when she figured out that housework was boring, she began to notice that box more and more. She took to dusting it every morning. She polished the jewels every afternoon. One day Epi came home from work early, and when he saw her fondling that box, he shoved it in the closet. "Whooeee, Pandy honey, don't mess with that box! That box is trouble with a capital T and that rhymes with P and that stands for … uh … for …"

"Pooey!" said Pandora. She wasn't scared of that box. She was curious about that box. And she went on being curious. As soon as Epi went back to work, she took that box out of the closet and put it on the coffee table. She read the tag under the lock again: UNDER PENALTY OF LAW—DO NOT REMOVE.

And she said to herself, "How come I can't open that box? This here is *my* box. What could possibly be in there that Papa Zeus wouldn't want me to see?"

She commenced to stare at that box for hours each day. Her eyes would glaze over and she would even talk to that box. She began to look just like a soap opera addict. But that box held more troubles than a whole year's worth of "The Guiding Light" and "The Young and the Restless" combined. Before long, Pandora was plumb eat up with curiosity. Why couldn't she just remove the lock, lift the lid, and have a tiny peek? She wouldn't take anything out of the box or lose it, for crying out loud!

Well, like I said before, Pandora was smart. So she finally figured it out. "Papa Zeus put that sign on the box so nobody else would mess with it *but* me. After all, it was my present," she thought. "It's a lousy job," she chuckled, "but somebody's got to do it." She ran out to the garage and got a crowbar. She popped off the lock, and lifted up the lid, and ... well, that's when it all hit the fan!

All the stuff that makes our lives miserable to this day came jumping out of that box: sickness, old age, anger, envy, and lust. Racism, sexism, terrorism, and tourism. Nepotism, alcoholism, plagiarism, and TV evangelism. War and bombs and the IRS. Cholesterol, hemorrhoids, PMS, and the heartbreak of psoriasis. Oh yes, all of that stuff and much, much more.

But there was one little misfit down in the bottom of the box. Her name was Hope. She really didn't want to join the others, but she felt an obligation to take a flying leap just the same. Instead, she took a chance, and yelled out, "Pandora, honey, you think you could shut that lid? Otherwise, girl, I'm outta here!"

Just in the nick of time, Pandora got a grip on herself and slammed down the lid and Hope was kept safe in the box.

Under the circumstances, considering she was framed and all, I think Pandora did the best she could for us. You can blame her for your troubles if you want to, but when you're down and out and nothing else seems to help, just remember: there's always Hope. She's still there ... deep inside ... waiting for you when you need her.

BOB CHURA

TOM McDERMOTT is a native Texan of Irish descent who blends rich musical instrumentation with original lyrics, humor, and folklore to create a unique experience in storytelling. He is a member of the award-winning Celebration Shop, Inc., and a past president of the Tejas Storytelling Association. He performed as a tale trader at the first-ever Texas Storytelling Festival and was invited back as a featured teller the next year. This lively teller, who often accompanies himself on guitar, ukelele, drum, or hurdy-gurdy, evokes in performance strong images that are at once infectious and healing.

The Caged Bird

TOM McDERMOTT

This Sufi teaching tale is attributed to the thirteenth-century Sufist poet/mystic Rumi. The story strikes a deep and resonant chord with me as I think of my grandmother, Eloise Snyder, who reluctantly gave up a blossoming career as a coloratura with the New York Civic Opera to return home and fulfill the role of wife and mother. That sacrifice followed her the rest of her life in personal poems that reflected the feeling of being in a cage with "clipped wings." I have adapted the fable widely and added some complex guitar chording to augment the mood of the tale. A signature story of mine since 1986, the tale is a powerful exploration of personal hope and the effects of our actions on one another.

There was once a fine merchant in Persia. He had a beautiful caged bird with deep blue feathers and gray-tipped wings. All day long she would sing the same song.

> *"I want to fly away free from my cage.*
> *I want to find a way free from this place!"*
> *She would sing strong and clear, for any bird flying near,*
> *"I want to be free, free some day!"*

One afternoon, the merchant approached the cage and told his bird, "Tomorrow I will be traveling to your homeland deep in the forest to buy goods that I can bring home to sell. I thought perhaps I could give your friends or family a message, if I saw them."

"Take a message?" she cried in disbelief. "Why take a message when you could set me free? I could go there myself. My friends would never worry about me again!"

But the merchant rapped the side of the cage and shouted, "Never! I would not think of letting you go. I caught you to keep you, so you had better learn to like it here!"

The angry merchant turned to leave, when the bird said, "Then at least give my friends and family a message. Tell them that I am here, in a cage."

Well, the merchant agreed to do that much. And the next morning he packed up his horses, readied his small caravan, and set out for his bird's homeland deep in the forest.

Now the merchant traveled many days and bought many goods to sell. But in all his traveling he never saw any birds that looked like his own. Frustrated and tired, he decided to give up the search and return home. As he reached the edge of the forest, he suddenly heard a bird singing a strangely familiar song. High up in one of the trees he saw a bird with deep blue feathers and gray-tipped wings. So he called out the message he had been given: "You have a friend who is in a cage in my home. She wanted you to know that."

Then he turned and was about to spur his horse when he heard an odd flutter of wings. He looked back to see that the blue-feathered bird had fallen lifeless to the ground. When he nudged the lifeless body with his sandal, the bird did not move a feather and it did not make a sound. The merchant suddenly realized the power of words and that his message had killed the bird by breaking its heart. Wondering how to break the news to his own bird, he slowly made his way home.

In his home, the caged bird could hardly wait for the merchant's return. She could only think of the good news he would be bringing, and so she sang ...

> "I want to fly away free from my cage.
> I want to find a way free from this place!"
> She would sing strong and clear, for any bird flying near,
> "I want to be free, free some day!"

With her cage by the window, the bird suddenly saw the merchant returning in the distance. His horses were packed with goods she recognized from her homeland. But as he drew near, her heart filled with sadness; for the expression on his face was not happy at all, but troubled. Soon the merchant entered the house and told her the bad news.

"I am sorry," he said, "but as soon as I found one of your friends, I told them of the message you gave to me. No sooner had I said the words than your friend fell lifeless to the ground, dead from a broken heart. I wish I had better news to tell you."

The merchant turned away from the cage. When he heard an odd flutter of feathers, he turned to see his own bird had fallen lifeless from her perch to the cage floor. The merchant shook the cage. But the bird did not move a feather and she would sing no more. And the merchant realized, once again, the power of his words; for his message had obviously killed both birds.

He opened up the cage door, lifted out the lifeless body of the bird, and tossed it through an open window.

At that moment, the bird suddenly spread her wings and flew away. When she was high in a nearby tree and out of the merchant's reach, she shouted back to him. "You see, the news that you brought to me was not bad news. It was glad news, because the words of my friends and the actions they took have now taught me how to find my freedom."

As she flew off, the merchant could clearly hear her song.

"Now I will fly away free from my cage.
Now I have found a way free from this place!"She sang loud and
she sang clear, for any bird passing near,
"I am free, free at last, this day!"

The once-caged bird flew off to her wooded homeland, where she found her friend. And they flew off together.

A Curious Legacy

TOM McDERMOTT

Ireland is full of tricksters and pranksters and those locals always ready to catch a visitor off-guard with a tale or a joke. Such was the case with the boat keeper my wife and I met on the Lough Ree boat dock in 1988. I have been telling the story ever since: Seamus's skill and outright boldness hit close to home; I couldn't help seeing a connection. McDermott Castle can still be seen in Lough Ree, just south of Roscommon, Ireland.

One of my warm discoveries from a recent trip to Ireland with my wife, Linda, was the general familiarity with which people there regarded the name McDermott. Not once did we have to repeat the name or spell it when introducing ourselves. But when we introduced ourselves to the bed and breakfast hostess in Dublin, I was unprepared for her enthusiasm.

"Well now," she laughed, "I suppose you're on your way to Roscommon."

"No, why?" I asked.

"Why, because your very heritage began outside Roscommon at Lough Ree. Did you not know? Such a fine representation of Irish beauty, imagination, and wit!"

We asked for directions and left early the next morning.

Lough Ree lies about seventy-five kilometers west of Dublin. Still, navigating the thick fog and the winding roads, we did not arrive until mid-morning. The park was a mystical wonder—a thick mist sat but a foot off the still surface of the water, like a thinly veiled curtain. There was a stone lodge along the shore of the lake. But the place seemed closed and empty with no one around.

"What a disappointment," Linda sighed.

There was a concrete boat dock with small rowboats tied on both sides and a small shack on the end. We could just make out the shape of a small island in the mist with a castle tower rising above the trees. So I looked quickly around once more and, noting the boats were not locked, I suggested, "Hey, let's take one of these across the lake! We'll pay for them if anyone shows up."

Linda wasn't so sure about it, but I urged her on into the boat. I was just untying it from the post when we both heard a door squeak open on the other side of the boathouse. A short, bandy-legged and ruddy-complected man rushed around the corner toward us. He looked to be as old as the Lough itself, his eyes leering distrustfully.

He squinted his right eye and raised his left brow. "And just what would you be doing with me boats?"

I was a little offended by the sharp tone of his voice. "I'm sorry, I didn't know they were yours."

"Well, tell me then. Are they yours?"

"No, of course not," I laughed. I could hear the sarcasm in his voice and knew we had overstepped our bounds. "We were only going to borrow the boat 'til someone showed up."

The old man stepped forward and pointed a bony finger in my face. "You were going to steal it, you mean?"

"Nonsense," I countered. "Where would I take it?"

"I was asking meself the same question."

I pulled the boat up closer to the dock and tied it to the post. Taking the man aside, I added, "Look, I was just trying to appease my wife. It was all her idea ..."

"Now there you have it," he laughed. "History repeatin' itself and you're blamin' the woman. You're a shameful lad. Tell me your name."

"Of course," I reached out with my hand. "I'm Tom McDermott, and this is my ..."

The man's face suddenly took on an look of amazement. "So, that's it. You're a McDermott. Then I might have known you to be a thief."

"Excuse me?" I asked. "What do you mean by that?"

"Saints, lad. Do you not know where you are?" He pointed across to the island with the tower and added, "That is McDermott Castle—well, what's left of the place."

"You're kidding!" I exclaimed.

"Now," he said with an indignant expression, "why would I lie to you when I don't even know you, yet?"

The old man quickly got in the boat and took us across to see the castle, enlightening us as to its history. He told us how the first McDermotts arrived in the area as underlords to the King of Connacht nearly a thousand years ago. "In their prime," he smiled, "they ruled with a fair and kind hand. But as one generation gave way to the next, frugality and temperance gave way to sloth and more creative endeavors. They became a rueful bunch, and in the mid-1800s, they burnt the place down during a party!"

When we got back to the dock, he got out of the boat and squinted suspiciously at me again. "You know, you being a thief and all, surely you have heard of a distant relative of yours—Seamus McDermott?"

In point of fact, I told him, I had not. And our impromptu guide was into the story before we could stop him.

"Seamus McDermott grew up in Roscommon in the late 1870s. An infamous young lad, his family underwent a time of great hunger and need. So Seamus took to using his imagination to find his work. In no time of it, the lad became a fine representation of the enterprising spirit. He became a thief—a pickpocket, actually.

"Now just where he learned his trade is not known. Some would argue he received his training at the hands of more skilled guides at the 'Lifting Institute' in the back of O'Malley's Pub. But Seamus would have nothing to do with the likes of such cutpurses and scoundrels. No, I believe with Seamus, his talent was a gift from the Almighty. It seemed to come to him so naturally. Even as a baby, he was taking things that belonged to others."

I interrupted our guide here. "Now, just a minute. What's so unusual about a baby taking things? They all do that."

"Indeed, 'tis a sad state we're coming to," quipped the old man. "Now, if you'll let me finish. You see, with pickpocketing, Seamus found he could combine all his talents and interests into an orchestration of movement and dance. Like an eagle, the lad would search for a naive passerby, their purse or pocketbook loosely at their side or their coat pockets wide and baggy. He could see how some folks' minds were cluttered with notions and anxieties. Then, like a shadow, Seamus would move in behind his prey with greatest stealth, mirroring their every move: to the left, to the right, arms swinging up. Seamus would suddenly bump the person off balance and catch him with his left arm while his right hand quickly searched and removed the treasure.

"It was gratifying work—the victims always thanked him before he moved on!

"On one of his more creative ventures, Seamus donned a wig and dress, stuffed a round pillow in the front, and entered Sunday mass as a pregnant young girl. The dress sleeves, you see, were stuffed as well and placed on his belly, while his real arms awaited opportunity beneath slits in the sides of his dress. As the people around him would stand up from their pews, Seamus would stand and lean up against one of them, in obvious need of support. Then, he picked their pockets and purses!

"Realizing he must be the best pickpocket in all of Ireland, he decided to ply his trade in the big city of Dublin itself. Day after day he stood at Dublin Square just outside the stone archway into Trinity College. Doctors and professors passed this way and that, dressed in their finest and each of them in such hurries to get here or there. It was easy pickin' for Seamus, who bumped and pushed and pulled whatever he could—pocketbooks, coins, and gold watches. And to his mind, what was he doing but relieving these busy people of a bit of their weighty burdens!

"All was going well as ever, until one late morning Seamus felt a sudden bump. His own pocket being picked! He looked down the way and there he saw a smartly dressed red-headed woman swaying back and forth, his own pocketbook swinging boldly in her right hand.

"He chased the lass down and caught up with his pocket book. 'Now,' he decried, 'if I am the finest pickpocket in all of Ireland, how is it you just picked me own pocket?'

"To which she sweetly replied, 'Simple—you're not.'

"To be sure, Seamus was taken by her looks. But being the purest of entrepreneurs, he was taken more by her talent. So he introduced himself and then quickly asked her to marry him. 'After all,' he exclaimed, 'with our talents combined we could raise a race of pickpockets!'

"Now Jenny—that was the lass's name—she agreed the proposal was most pragmatic. So the two were married straight away. Now what might be said about these two thieving lovebirds? Well, a happier and more talented couple you never did meet. They were everywhere together. Picking pockets here, pulling out watches there. Why, the way they had learned to combine their skills by day, and exchange their talents at night, it was only a matter of time before something was to come of it all. And something did come of it, a baby it was—the first of what they hoped to be many distinguished pickpockets.

"But tragedy struck, and the Devil himself must have had his hand in it. The midwife called Seamus inside just as she was about to lift up the newborn baby. 'It's a boy, Seamus, a fine, strapping ...'

"And then she stopped short. Horror-stricken they all were as she handed the baby over; for the lad's right arm was frozen up stiff against its little chest and would not move. Even his tiny fist was clenched tight.

"When Jenny tried to move the little arm, the baby gave out such a cry of pain that she immediately let go. Well, Seamus's heart sank straight to the floor—there went their whole retirement, right before their eyes!

"For the next six months, they took the little lad to every doctor in Dublin. But they all said the same thing: 'I don't understand. The circulation to the baby's arm is fine. Everything seems in order.' They would try to move the arm, and the lad would let out that terrible cry of pain. All the doctors would say after that was, 'I'm sorry for you.'

"Hoping for a miracle, they took the baby to a priest. This clever priest actually recognized the celebrated pickpocket's voice from previous confessions and informed the worried parents he had an idea as to the cure for the lad. The holy cleric reached into his robe and pulled out a shiny gold pocketwatch, which he then dangled before the infant's eyes. What do you think but that the infant's eyes snapped over to see the object and began to sparkle with excitement. Seamus and Jenny watched in amazement as the little lad's right arm began to loosen ever so slowly and, like a pendulum, move in time with it. Back and forth, back and forth, closer and closer that right arm moved toward the shiny object. It was the miracle the proud parents had been hoping for. Their hearts began to lift when, suddenly, the baby reached out, opened his little hand to grab the watch, and, to everyone's great delight, out of the baby's hand fell the midwife's ring!"

Linda and I laughed for some time as our clever guide began to secure the boat to the dock. He assured us that the tale was thoroughly true and that the little boy was the only child Seamus and Jenny had. "He grew up to be a fine pickpocket, he did."

The old man stood up and adjusted his cap. "Don't you know, other McDermotts have gone on to more respectable, though not so completely unrelated vocations since then—politics, advertising"—then addressing me directly—"and boat snatching!" He stopped talking and squinted that right eye at me as he quickly began inspecting his pockets. Then finding everything in apparent order, he smiled at us, turned, and went back inside the boathouse.

The Old Man's Thief

TOM McDERMOTT

The beauty of a teaching tale is often its ability to say much with little and to leave an indelible image of meaning in our minds. This simple Zen tale does just that. I first read this tale in Paul Reps' collection, Zen Flesh, Zen Bones. *The book—and story—was recommended to me by a friend shortly before he died of bone cancer some years ago. We had been talking over the phone about the highs and lows of his career as a musical artist. I asked how he was able to maintain any sense of creativity in the midst of a battle with cancer. He responded with the story. Years later, I adapted the tale lyrically and added ukelele accompaniment. It is a story that continues to speak to me often.*

There was an old man who lived a simple sort of life,
  In a small wooden hut, on a hillside midway up,
a mountain path nearby.
And every evening he would sit and watch the distant sway of treetops,
Silhouettes against the vast and starry sky.

But in the morning, the sun would rise;
    and the old man would open his eyes
And smiling out upon the valley exclaim, "All of this is mine!"

Then one night he heard a very strange, suspicious sound,
The crunch and crackle, crackle and crunch of leaves upon the ground.
And he awoke to meet a thief wielding a knife and wearing a scowl!
"Give me all your money, and all you have," cried the thief.
The old man simply smiled and said, "I haven't even food for you to eat.
But since you've come such a long, long way to go home empty-handed,
    At least let me offer you something, the clothes off my back, for what you've
        demanded."

Well, the brazen thief tore up the hut to see what he could find in it.
And the less he found, the more he grew angrier by the minute.
"You're a fool, old man! Now give me what you have, or else."
So the man removed his clothes and gave them to the thief
Who was by now beside himself!

In the brilliance of a full moon the old man stood there shivering, as he
watched the thief go down
To the crackle and crunch, crunch and crackle of leaves upon the ground.
"Poor friend," the old man began to muse. "If only he had not left here so
soon.
Perhaps then, I could have offered him my view of this beautiful moon."

DAVID FITZGERALD

LYNN MORONEY is a full-time freelance storyteller and author with a number of fine published works. A background in the sciences and arts gives shape to her twenty-five years of storytelling that include performances, workshops, and visiting author programs across the United States and Mexico. Of her work Lynn says, "The stories I tell are a celebration of my love for the cosmos. They are an expression of my Native American and Anglo-American ancestry, and an affirmation of my roots on the windswept prairie of Oklahoma. In story I believe we can explore and extol our world—a world filled with people and places that resonate great stories for us all." She lives in Oklahoma City, Oklahoma.

The Star Husband

LYNN MORONEY

While tales of celestial suitors are told the world over, the story of The Star Husband belongs to Native America. My retelling is based on a Blackfoot version, told by Wolf-head to Clark Wissler in 1903. In the resonance of this poignant tale, we are invited to enter into the story, to explore its many other versions, to bathe in the rich mythic images found in Native American oral literature, and to view the "Fixed Star" with a new awareness. For more information, see Star Legends Among the American Indians *by Clark Wissler (New York: The American Museum of Natural History, Guide Leaflet No. 91, 1936) and* Literary Types and Dissemination of Myths *by Gladys A. Reichard (Journal of American Folklore 34: 269-305).*

One summer night two girls decided to sleep outside. They left the place where all the others were camped and walked until they came to a hill. They made their beds, and after they had lain down, they began to watch the stars. As the sky grew darker, the stars grew in number and brightness.

"These stars are beautiful," said one girl.

"Oh, look! One of the stars just fell," said the other.

"There in the south is a red star," said one.

"And just there, there is a yellow star," said the other.

With the appearance of each new star the girls grew more delighted. They agreed that sleeping outside was a good idea, for never had they seen so beautiful a night.

In time, one of the maids noticed one special star. "Sister, see that star," she said, "that white star just over there? That is my favorite star. I wish that star could be my husband. If I married that star, I could go way into the sky and live with the stars."

The girls gazed at the stars for a while longer, but the night had worn on, and in time they fell asleep—sound asleep under a sky filled with stars.

The next day, on their way back to camp, the girls found a berry patch. They started gathering berries, and the girl who had wished for a husband wandered off. As soon as she was alone, she heard a sound. Looking up, she saw a young man standing before her. He wore a white feather in his hair, and his vest and moccasins were beaded with white and crystal beads that sparkled and glimmered like the stars.

"Do not be afraid," he said. "Last night you wished to marry the white star. I am that white star. I am White Morning Star, and I have come for you. Marry me, and we shall live in the sky world."

All fear left the girl, and she gave her hand to the young man. At once, they began their journey to the sky.

When the other girl discovered that her friend was missing, she ran back to the camp. She told the girl's mother and all the people that she had no idea what had happened to her friend. "We were gathering berries and she just disappeared," she said. Then she began to weep. The people in camp could not understand what could have happened, and for a long time afterward, they waited for the girl's return.

In the meantime, the young couple reached the sky. The girl noticed how much the sky world was like the world below. There were rivers and streams, rolling hills, trees, wildflowers, animals and birds, and all manner of good roots and berries.

The Star Husband presented his new bride to his parents. His father was the Sun, and his mother was the Moon. Moon was the first to speak, saying, "We are pleased that you have come to live with us, and to have you for our daughter." Moon liked her new daughter-in-law, and wanted her to be happy. Then Moon set about teaching the young bride many special things about the sky land.

One day Moon gave her daughter-in-law a magic digging stick. "With this stick you will be sure to find many kinds of roots. Find them and always take as many as you please, but heed this warning: there is one root that you must never dig." Then Moon took the young wife to a place where many prickly bushes and thorns grew. Right in the center there was growing one green plant. "Daughter ... do you see that turnip plant? You must never dig for that turnip. You must never pull it from where it is growing. Do you understand?"

The bride said she understood, and she and Moon went on their way.

Time passed. The Star Husband and his young wife were very happy. She learned much about the sky world. Each day she went forth to gather berries and roots, and always she was careful not to dig around the forbidden plant. More time passed, and the happy couple had a fine baby boy. The Sky People brought him gifts and shared their joy.

The baby grew, and the young mother continued each day to gather food, but over time she changed. Instead of avoiding the place where the turnip grew, she passed by it each day. She began having strange thoughts: *I wonder why I cannot have that turnip. Perhaps Moon is just being selfish, and does not want me to have anything that tastes so good.*

Each day it was the same. She would sometimes stare at the turnip plant for long periods of time. Soon the young mother began to brood over the plant, and wondered, "What kind of turnip plant can it be? What secret does it hold?"

One day, when her baby was at the age when he could sit by himself, the maid again went to the place where the plant was growing. She sat her son down, and this time, slowly and carefully, very carefully, she began to dig around the plant with her digging stick. She poked and dug until the ground was soft. Then she reached down and pulled the turnip up and out of where it was growing. *Whooosh!* A rush of air came from the hole. She then looked down through the hole, and to her surpise, she could see the earth below—tall grasses, rolling hills, many buffalo—and she could see the lodges of her people.

That night when her sky family saw the turnip, they scolded her, and Moon asked, "Did you see anything unusual when you pulled the turnip from where it grew?"

The young wife answered, "Oh, nothing unusual, just the Earth, and the lodges of my people."

The Star Husband gasped. "No! You do not know what you have done! Now that you have looked again upon the Earth, you cannot stay here in the sky. You must leave at once. You must take our son and return to your people. When you reach Earth, you must not let our son touch the Earth for fourteen days. If you do, he will turn first into a little puff ball of seeds, then he will turn into a star. He will not move through the sky, as do other stars. He will remain always in one place."

The Sun Father called one of the sky men to help the mother and child down to the earth. The sky man took a rope made of spiderwebs and, tying the mother and child to one end, he slowly let them down through the turnip hole.

Now down on earth, some boys were playing, and they saw the young woman and her child coming down from the sky. Soon she was hanging above the center of camp. One of the boys recognized her and cried out, "Look! It is the girl who disappeared while she was gathering berries." All of the people in the camp ran to her. Everyone was glad to see her, especially her mother, who quickly took her daughter and grandson to her lodgings.

The young woman told her mother all about the sky world, and for the first thirteen days, everything went well. The young mother was ever so watchful over her child, careful never to let him touch the ground.

Then on the fourteenth day, the grandmother asked her daughter to fetch some water. The girl cautioned, "Mother, while I am gone, be sure to watch my son every moment. He must not leave his bed of blankets, for he must not so much as even touch the ground." Then the girl hurried off to gather water.

The grandmother did not understand why her grandson should not touch the earth. She watched over the child for a while, but from time to time, she looked away. Then, while her back was turned, the baby boy crawled to the edge of the blankets. Just as the grandmother turned back around, she saw the boy place one little hand upon the ground. Quickly, she swept him up and placed him back in the center of the blanket.

But it was too late. Without a sound, the baby boy crawled inside the pile of blankets that had made his bed ...

The mother returned with the water, and not seeing the boy, she was filled with fear. "Where is my son?" she whispered.

"He's down inside the blankets," said the grandmother.

The mother rushed over to the bed and began pulling the blankets away, one after another. She did not find her son. All she found was a little ball of puffy white seeds. She knew what had happened. Slowly she picked up the little puff ball and placed it close to her heart.

That evening the mother went to the top of a small hill. It was the same hill where, many moons before, she had wished for a husband. She watched as, one by one, the stars came into the sky. High in the northern sky, in the place where she had pulled up the turnip, there was a new star. The young mother knew that that little star was her son. That night and all the star-filled nights from then until the day she died, the mother of the star looked into the sky and sent her love to her son.

It was in this way that the fixed star, the star-that-does-not-move came to be. The star is still there, for the stars go on ... and on ...

NICOLE KROEGER

GAYLE ROSS is a direct descendant of Chief John Ross, Principal Chief of the Cherokee Nation during the infamous Trail of Tears. Since 1979, she has traveled the country telling Native American stories at schools, libraries, colleges, and festivals. She has recorded two audiotapes of Cherokee stories, and her stories have appeared on two educational videotapes. Her collection of Cherokee rabbit stories, *How Rabbit Tricked Otter*, is published by Harper-Collins Publishers. Gayle lives with her husband, Reed Holt, and her two children, Alan and Sarah, in the Texas Hill Country town of Fredericksburg.

The Bird That Was Ashamed of Its Feet

GAYLE ROSS

"The Bird That Was Ashamed of Its Feet" is a traditional Cherokee tale. I first found it in a small booklet entitled Legends and Folklore of the Cherokees *compiled by C.W. "Dub" West and published by the Muskogee Publishing Company of Muskogee, Oklahoma. The story delighted me because I have very big feet! Whenever I tell it, children seem to love it, perhaps because they all have something about their appearance that they find distressing.*

This is what the old people told me when I was a child, about the days when the world was new and all creatures still spoke the same language. Now, in those days, there was a bird called Meadowlark, whose feet grew so big that he was ashamed of them. While the other birds flew through the air and sang in the treetops, Meadowlark hid himself in the tall grass where no one could see him. He spent all his time staring down at his big feet and worrying about them.

"Provider must have made a terrible mistake," thought Meadowlark, turning his feet this way and that. No matter how he looked at them, all Meadowlark could see was how big his feet were. "Perhaps Creator thought this would be a funny joke to play," said Meadowlark. "I'm sure anyone who saw my big feet would laugh at them, but I do not think this is funny at all." And so Meadowlark continued to hide himself away in the tall grass.

One day Grasshopper was going about his business, making his way through the tall grass, when he bumped smack into Meadowlark, sitting on the ground and staring sadly at his feet.

"What are you doing here?" asked Grasshopper. "You are not one of those birds who live on the ground! You should be in the treetops with the other birds. Why do you not fly and sing as they do?"

"I am ashamed," answered Meadowlark. "These feet that Provider gave me are so big and ugly that I am afraid that everyone will laugh at me!"

Grasshopper looked down at Meadowlark's feet, and his eyes grew big with amazement. It was true; Meadowlark's feet were huge! Grasshopper did his best not to smile; he did not want to hurt Meadowlark's feelings.

129

Finally he said, "Well, it is true that your feet are perhaps a bit larger than those of other birds your size. But Creator does not make mistakes. If your feet are big, you may be sure that they will be useful to you someday. Big feet will not keep you from flying. Big feet will not stop you from singing. You are a bird and you should act like one!" And Grasshopper went on about his business.

After Grasshopper had gone on his way, Meadowlark sat and thought about his words. "Perhaps he is right," said Meadowlark. "The size of my feet cannot change the sound of my voice or the power of my wings. I should use the gifts Creator gave me." And so Meadowlark took Grasshopper's advice and flew out to sing. He landed in the top of a tree, threw back his head, and let his song pour from his throat. Meadowlark could really sing! Piercingly sweet and beautiful, the liquid notes of Meadowlark's song spread through the forest.

One by one, the animal people stopped what they were doing and gathered to listen to Meadowlark's voice. Raccoon, Possum, and Skunk; Deer, Bear, and Wolf; even Rabbit paused in his scurrying about to listen in wonder to this marvelous singer. The other birds flocked around Meadowlark, listening. Even Mockingbird fell silent, entranced by the melody that Meadowlark sang.

When Meadowlark began to sing, he forgot everything else, even his big feet. He closed his eyes and lost himself in the joyful song Creator had given him. When at last he finished his song and looked around, there were all the other birds and animals, staring at him. With a rush of shame, Meadowlark remembered his feet. Thinking that the others were staring at him because he was so ugly, Meadowlark flew back down to the tall grass and hid. And this time he would not come out.

Not very far from the tall grass where Meadowlark hid, there was a wheat field planted by the Human Beings. Now there was a Quail who had made her nest and laid her eggs in the middle of this wheat field. Every day she sat on her nest and waited for her eggs to hatch. As the wheat grew ripe and her eggs had still not hatched, Quail began to worry. Sure enough, one afternoon she heard the people talking about how they were going to come out and cut the wheat the very next day. Quail knew that her nest would be trampled and her eggs crushed, and she began to cry.

Now Grasshopper heard Quail crying, and he came to see what was wrong. "The men are coming to cut the wheat," Quail cried, "and my family will die!"

Suddenly Grasshopper had an idea. "Wait here," he told Quail. "I think I know someone who can help."

Grasshopper hurried to find Meadowlark. "Quail needs help to move her family," said Grasshopper, "and I think your big feet are the answer."

When Meadowlark heard of Quail's trouble, he agreed at once to try to help. He flew to Quail's nest. There he found that his big feet were just the right size to pick up Quail's eggs. Very carefully, Meadowlark lifted Quail's eggs and flew with them to the safety of the tall grass. There Quail built a new nest, and it was not long before the eggs hatched. As Meadowlark watched Quail tending her beautiful babies, he thought to himself, "My feet may be big and ugly, but they did a good thing. I should not be ashamed of them!"

And so Meadowlark flew out of the tall grass, back to the treetops where he began to sing. He is singing to this day, and his song is still so beautiful that everyone stops to listen.

VALERIE ADAMS

After a brief stint running heavy equipment, JAY STAILEY took a job with the Houston Public Library as a resident storyteller on the HPL's Children's Carousel. His storytelling hasn't stopped since. He has worked in elementary schools in Texas and South America as a teacher, and is currently a principal in Houston's Goose Creek Independent School District. His stories are often spiced with singing and guitar accompaniment, a pinch of juggling, and maybe even a spin on a unicycle. Jay first shared stories at the Texas Storytelling Festival in 1990. He lives with his wife and two daughters outside of Houston on the island of Clear Lake Shores.

The Giant Cockroaches
of Clear Lake Shores

JAY STAILEY

This is the first of the stories from my "Short Tales, Tall Tales, and Tales of Medium Stature" collection that I put down on paper. I wrote it for my mother, whose Midwestern sensibilities were so shocked at her first sighting of a Gulf Coast wood roach that she would have believed even this tale! This was the first story I ever told at the Texas festival.

There on the island at City Hall, they got an old scrapbook of city history. I looked it up in the scrapbook, and it is just as I suspicioned: our city's twenty-fifth birthday and sure enough, this has been the damnedest year on record. Some say it's because of the city elections, but I think you can blame it on the winter. You see, we didn't get a hard freeze this year. We didn't even get a semi-hard freeze. It takes a semi-hard freeze to catch an even chance against the skeeters and the fleas. And then there is a certain amount of human orneriness that gets nipped in the bud by a semi-hard freeze. So by city election time, the end of March, instead of that orneriness just popping through the surface to take a shower in the spring rains, it was well-grown and just raring to burst into full blossom.

The citizens of the Shores were showing their typical apathetic response to election time. No one had thought much about either running for office or caring who was. When the city paper landed at the foot of the drive, those that got it before the rain blobbed the words all together found out that three of their neighbors were warmly contesting two open council seats, and with Mayor Laramore not seeking re-election, a city councilman was running for his open office unopposed.

Ron Gardner was the fella's name who was going to be the next mayor. And on meet-the-candidates night, Wednesday before our Saturday election, in a very short period of time, Ron managed to agitate, insult, and generally irritate about two-thirds of the electorate present. That included just about everyone but his family and a few very close friends. And some

133

say they were pretty teed off, too. It takes a lot to prod our citizens to action. But later that night the islanders discovered party politics. There was this party, you see, over at Mayor Laramore's house, and about ten o'clock the party politics began.

Laramore said, "You know, someone ought to be runnin' against Gardner. Shoot, then we could vote against Ron, even if the other guy was somebody no-count."

That seemed to those present like a splendid idea. After everyone withdrew his own name from consideration, someone mentioned George Keebler.

"Yeh, let's run George." And so it was decided. Except no one bothered to ask George. They just started promoting him as write-in candidate.

George Keebler lives three houses down from me. He's seventy-six, bald on the top, gray around the edges, and listing slightly to the port side. My wife swears he's kin to the Keebler elves of cookie fame, and until recently, I thought she'd been joking. George thought they were joking about a write-in campaign until folks kept coming by shouting "good luck" to him as he worked in his garden. People had never shown much interest in his garden before, so he assumed they must be talking about the election. But Mr. Keebler had been around awhile, and he knew no write-in candidate had won an election for mayor in Galveston County for as long as he could recall. So he slept quite comfortably each night until election day.

As I said, it's been a strange year, and we shouldn't have been surprised when the results were tallied. George not only won, he won by a landslide. Next day I was down talking to him while he pulled weeds in his garden. A neighbor rode by and shouted out congratulations. George waved and said thanks, but to me he added, "Don't know whether they should be offering congratulations or condolences."

It didn't take long for me to find out what he meant. No one's quite sure where the cockroaches came from. Don't get me wrong. We live near the water on the steamy Gulf Coast, we've always had roaches. But none like these. I saw the winner of some "Biggest Cockroach" contest on David Letterman one night. That thing looked like a midget compared to the ones that came to the island in mid-May. Ricky Joe's cousin sailed in from Florida about then, and some folks blame him for bringing over a slew of them Caribbean roaches we'd been hearing about. One of them engineer fellas from NASA who lives down on Hawthorne claimed that it had to do with the shift in the jet stream … or possibly the hole in the ozone layer. Brother Parker shouted out at the city council meeting in June that it was all because of the way the island residents (brothers and sisters, he called us) was living in sin by not attending his Sunday morning services at the Holy Waters of the Bay Pentecostal Church. Me, I figured it to be just another case of some orneriness that didn't get nipped in the bud by a winter freeze.

Whatever it was, them roaches were big ones. Three, four, some of them five inches long. And only on the island. Didn't seem to be bothering the folks in Kemah or Seabrook. Lucky for us they weren't carnivores—though Miss Vanerson claimed a group of them carried away her cat one morning in broad daylight. In the beginning the city contracted out to Orkin, and then Big Tex Pest control, but it soon became clear that the problem was too big for them to handle. Seemed like for every roach we found dead there were two more to take its place. The state health department came to help out but decided the roaches were so big that the situation should be turned over to Parks and Wildlife. Parks and Wildlife sent out a ranger who only stayed for about five minutes. He left after one look at those roaches, promising to be back the minute the legislature passed the new budget.

One good thing was that most of the darn roaches were too big to sneak in the houses. But then the smaller ones started slipping through cracks and opening the doors for the bigger ones. They were eating everything that was wood, which meant most everyone's homes, trees, and a whole mess of very expensive boats. By the end of June, the city council was meeting three, four times a week looking for an answer. And there was a goodly number of more citizens in attendance than ever came for a meet-the-candidates night. Mayor Keebler was beginning to feel some political pressure. He was the choice of the people, and now the people wanted action.

The council had advertised a $10,000 reward for anyone who could rid the island of roaches, and crazy nuts came out of the woodwork and swarmed over the island nearly as thick as the roaches. One fella had a plan for a roach hotel, multi-story, at the corner of Clear Lake Drive and Forest, but the council rejected it because it didn't meet standards of the building code. Another, had a plan that called for a limited evacuation of the island and several tons of dynamite brought in by barge. The mayor cast the deciding vote against that plan. By the first of July, the city was desperate. On July 2, at the fifteenth emergency session of the city council, a thin and pale stranger walked through the door and quietly announced that he could rid the city of its roaches.

The secretary didn't get in the minutes who first suggested it, and it is still a bone of contention with the councilmen, but she did note that there was unanimous agreement. Someone, however, did say, "Young fella, if you can rid this island of roaches we'll pay you one hundred thousand dollars."

The deal was struck quickly, as the desperation level was rising at an equal rate with the summer heat and the citizens' tempers. When the stranger proposed his solution, there was disappointment in the citizenry and a general consensus among the mayor and the honorable councilmen that there was little chance the reward would be paid.

"You see," he began in his quiet manner, "everything is susceptible to a tone, a pitch, or a combination of tones and pitches that can be used to gain complete control."

"Sorta like that new flea collar Winston Venner got for his dog," interrupted Councilman Blake. "Says the fleas can't tolerate the sound it gives off. Too high for us to hear though."

"Yeh, kinda like that dog whistle Captain Wacker used with his hounds when we went duck hunting in February," added Councilman Cole.

"It doesn't just work on animals," the stranger finally commented when the mayor wrestled the floor back his way.

"Oh, insects too, huh?" The councilmen nodded, smiling. But I noticed Mayor Keebler had a furrowed brow.

"Well, show us your stuff, boy," Councilman Cole said. "What you waiting for?"

With that, the skinny stranger pulled a little flute out of his pocket and shook it. It looked like one of them pennywhistles I saw some gal play down on the Strand at the Dickens Festival. And when he started to play I expected to hear no sound at all, but he was playing a little tune, and a catchy little tune at that. It was short, with kind of a jazzy Latin rhythm, and he played it over and over as he headed for the door. When we got outside someone shouted *"Olé!,"* and there was scattered laughter.

Then we thought we heard castanets. I figured it was Larry Smith's Peruvian wife, the girl he married when he was working down in South America. They live right there on Cedar, two doors down from city hall. But it turned out to be the sound of those little cockroach feet on the street pavement. They were coming in swarms, right down Clear Lake Boulevard, and Cedar and Birch, and around the corner at Shore Drive, thousands of them ... maybe millions.

A bunch of people ran back into city hall, but the stranger grabbed Buzz Laramore's oldest boy and they climbed into a rowboat, the skinny young man still playing that same catchy little Latin number. Out they went, down the channel and toward the bay, and when the roaches hit the water, well, they just kept going, swimming like crazy toward that rowboat. Buzz's boy said they kept going 'til they got well out into the bay.

Then all of the sudden, the stranger lowered the flute from his lips and stuck it in his pocket. Just as suddenly, the roaches quit swimming and, almost as one, sank into the bay. The kid said the wave from the rapid sinking of those bugs almost capsized the boat. As soon as they regained control, the stranger directed the boy to return to city hall.

By the time they got there, Mayor Keebler had called the sixteenth emergency meeting of city council to discuss fiscal liability. It didn't take a financial whiz to come to the conclusion that council had promised the entire year's city budget and several months into the next year, and that they were faced with an enormous cash flow problem. So as the stranger approached the door, council voted to offer the ten thousand originally budgeted—take it or leave it.

The stranger quietly insisted that in Texas, more so than any place else in the cosmos (Keebler's brow furrowed deeper), a deal was a deal, and he wished to be given his hundred grand so he could depart quietly.

"We appreciate your help," Mayor Keebler stated, "but ten thousand is all we can afford. You can take it or leave it."

After an extended silence, the mayor adjourned the meeting and those present shuffled by the stranger on their way to the door mumbling words of apology and appreciation, unable to meet his gaze.

"They'll be sorry," he said as the mayor reached to cut the lights.

And to my surprise I heard the mayor reply, "Yes, they will."

I went home feeling real uneasy, though it sure was nice to be able to walk my dog without hearing the roaches crunch under our feet. I was on my second trip around the island, and most all the lights were out, when I first heard it. It had to have been that stranger's flute, and the sound that floated around the island and over the water was a medley of the greatest, sweetest, and loneliest country and western songs ever penned. It was three-chord heartbreak music at its best, and it sounded better than Willie and Waylon. I wondered for a minute if he was planning on charming the young ladies of the island, but his revenge was far more devious than that.

I had just gotten to Bobby Ray James's house when I noticed some movement in the driveway. It was Bobby Ray's brand new Ford three-quarter-ton pickup, and it was backing out of the driveway without the engine running. It stopped, then started forward, passing me as it headed toward the bridge. That's when I noticed there weren't no driver. It was just like that Honda commercial on TV, the one with the eerie music where Burgess Meredith says that one night all America's cars were replaced by Honda Accords. Just like that commercial! After Bobby Ray's Ford went by, here come the Johnsons' Chevy, no engine running, no driver; then come Councilman Blake's little import, and another and another. Pickup truck after pickup truck.

I was still walking, just staring, when I turned on Ivy and saw Jesse Robbins' pickup with the camper on the back. Jesse's brother-in-law had been sleeping in the camper since early in the week when he had insulted his sister's cooking.

"No one talks to my wife that way," Jesse had hollered and banished Ray Bob to the trailer. Now he must have figured his sister's husband was gonna take him out of town in the dead of night and tell him never to come back. He opened the little window to the cab to try to talk him out of it, when he noticed there wasn't anybody at the wheel. He lit out the back of that camper in his boxer shorts and landed next to us in the ditch.

"Evening, Ray Bob," I said, as I turned the corner and headed toward the bridge. When I got up to the foot of the bridge I noticed the stranger had climbed into the bed of the pickup at the front of the line, still playing that country music. The front pickup started off the island, the rest followed. Pickup after pickup headed over the bridge and turned left toward Route 146. Old Nguyen, the Vietnamese shrimper that lives on Grove Street, had been coming home, and he pulled his Toyota longbed off into the cafe parking lot. He got out of his truck and stared in amazement. He was in such shock I don't even think he noticed when his truck fell right into line. At the very end of the procession was Mayor Keebler's old gold and white Dodge one-ton, and even though the engine wasn't running, it looked as if it was sputtering and missing, maybe on its last leg or about to run out of gas.

Well, I'm sure you read about the investigation in the big city papers. I believe the *Post* never did think it was more than just a tall tale. Most folks 'round here figure that the stranger was working with one of those car theft rings, the ones that strip down cars and trucks and sell the parts. Darren March, my next-door neighbor, he has a brother that works down on the docks at Barbour's Cut. His brother said that a German freighter had just unloaded a million dollars' worth of new Mercedes, and left in a hurry, ahead of schedule the morning after the stranger was on the island. The log at the port read that the freighter was empty. But Darren's brother said it was riding suspiciously low in the water.

The police were only able to recover one pickup truck. That was Mayor Keebler's. Needless to say, that didn't do much to strengthen his political base. Bobby Ray thinks he may have been involved with the car parts ring. My wife, however has a different theory.

The other afternoon she was having cookies and milk while Darren and I were talking about it. She dipped a cookie in her glass and said, "It was his cousins."

"Whose cousins?" I asked.

"The mayor's."

"What about 'em?"

"It was his cousins, the elves. The ones that make the cookies. They're the ones got the old man's truck back."

And you know, it could be. Been the damnedest year in the city's history. I hate to think what might happen next.

A Matter Between Friends

JAY STAILEY

One day, while we were walking around the island of Clear Lake Shores, my old buddy Bobby Haydocy told me this story. He claimed it happened in his neighborhood. Later, when he heard me tell this version, he admitted that it may indeed have happened in my neighborhood!

There on the island, Petee Boudreaux lives year round in a one-bedroom summer cottage on Juniper Street. Petee's not the oldest person on the island. Captain Okie holds that claim to fame. But Petee is easily pushing seventy-five—and feeling pretty good about it, too. Petee's retired now, but for years and years he trolled a shrimp boat 'round Galveston Bay.

Now Petee is a cat person. You probably know there are cat people and dog people, and Petee is one of the former. He tried having a dog once, but it just didn't work. He got one of those retrievers, the ones that are supposed to be good around the water. Petee'd take him down to the boat, and the dog would race up and down the pier whining and barking. Then Petee would get him on board and he'd race around the boat whining and barking. So he left him up on the dock, and Petee could hear that dog barking and whining until he was well away and couldn't see the shore anymore.

That's one reason why Petee's a cat person. As he's been heard to say, "They don't call 'em dog for nothing!" Cats never acted like dogs when they came on board Petee's shrimp boat. Even though cats hate water, they were good company for Petee once they got on the boat and found a place to be comfortable.

In the last couple of years when Petee was still shrimping, he had found him a black and white tom he named Fisher. Fisher would go down to the dock every morning with Petee, hop on board, and as soon as Petee cranked up that diesel engine, Fisher would jump up on the engine casing and stretch out. That engine would just hum and chug, and old Fisher thought it was purring just for him. And then his nose would start to itch, and he'd stretch out and crank up his own engine. He would just purr all over Galveston Bay.

After Petee retired, when the two of them didn't take the rowboat out fishing (Fisher was always awarded the first catch of the day), they could be seen out there on the front porch of the cottage. Petee would sit in the rocking chair and Fisher would jump up onto the window air-conditioning unit. When that unit kicked on and started humming, Fisher thought it was purring just for him, and he'd crank up his own little engine, stretch out, and dream he was out on the bay.

Philip Evans lives two doors down and across the street from Petee in one of those big houses built up on stilts. Philip's thirty-eight, and works in an upper-level management position for IBM across the lake at Big Blue's regional office. If you had told Philip twenty years ago, when he was a sophomore in college at Youngstown State, that he'd be in upper management with IBM before he was forty, he would have answered you with some sort of obscene gesture. Philip Evans planned to change the world, and he knows you don't do that in upper management at IBM. In fact, Philip is still not real comfortable with just how he got to be where he is at this point in his life. He does know, however, that he has made some decisions before all the facts were in, and has guessed right. It's a trait, he knows, that IBM likes in their upper management people.

Philip Evans is a dog person. You probably know that there are cat people and dog people, and Philip is one of the latter. Back in Youngstown, the Evanses had dogs long before they had Philip. And after they had Philip, they had more dogs as far back as Philip can remember. In the Evans family album there is, it seems, a dog in every picture, at every major occasion in the family history. So to Philip there is something just natural about having a dog. There is something that makes him feel kind of patriotic about walking a dog. So when Philip moved out of the apartment and into the house on Juniper, he got himself a Doberman pinscher and named him Max.

Now if you ask Philip if Max is pedigree, he'll admit he is. "But I didn't bother to get the papers," he's quick to add. And he didn't bother to have Max's ears cropped, or chopped, or whatever that is they do to those ears, because he didn't buy Max to show. He just bought him because it's right, somehow, to have a dog.

Petee and Philip are friends. There is something about the manner in which Petee is so comfortable with where he is and where he's been that intrigues Philip, and he's hoping that in this friendship he'll learn something more about that. When Philip goes over to Petee's to sit on the porch and have a beer, he leaves Max chained up in the back yard. Max is not a cat person.

Petee likes Philip all right, and is glad for this company. But the thing Petee likes best about Philip is his wife.

"Now Marie, she is some girl, and that's fo' sho'," Petee says. Marie is a Lafayette girl and met Philip when he was doing graduate work at LSU.

140

Even though she works in one of those big tall office buildings down in Houston, she hasn't forgotten how to make a great pot of filé gumbo. Nor has she forgotten about the "Southern hospitality that she was raised with." So Petee is often invited over to taste those Cajun treats. Now when he comes over to share that gumbo or crawfish etouffe, Fisher chooses to stay home. Fisher is not a dog person.

The good news came in November, I recall, of last year, when Marie found out that she was pregnant. They had put off starting a family in order to further their careers, but now was the time, and at their little celebration, they invited Petee over and let him know that they wanted him to be the godfather of their baby. I'm telling you, he was delighted with the news. He couldn't quit talking about it.

And it was right before Thanksgiving, that same month, when Philip once again amazed his bosses by making a decision before all the facts were in, and guessing right. They couldn't quit talking about it. So they decided to reward him with a long weekend for the two of them in Cancun. The happy couple left on the evening of the first Thursday in December, flying out of Hobby Airport on an unseasonably balmy day.

They enjoyed themselves thoroughly, and on Sunday evening, they flew back into Hobby. When they finally retrieved their luggage and car and got back on the island, it was well after dark. Marie went on up to bed, exhausted but glowing with memories of the trip and the thought of this wonderful new life to come. Philip had to unpack and tie up a few loose ends before going to bed.

He was sitting at the kitchen table doing some paperwork when Max scratched at the back door. He opened the door and looked down, seeing that Max had once again dragged home one of his "prizes." In the past he had brought in raccoons and possums, and once a nutria, one of those big water rats that live in the banks around the lake. Max set the carcass down on the back step, and Philip, not being able to identify it, turned on the light and rolled it over with the toe of his shoe. That's when he realized it was a cat.

Bending down to take a closer look, his heart sank. This wasn't just any cat: it was Fisher. Philip put his hands under the little body and carried it into the house. Geez, Fisher was dead all right, stone cold and caked in mud. Max must have dragged that cat all over the neighborhood, probably had it over in the dredging dirt down at the corner of North Shore Drive.

Philip took the kitchen towel and wiped at the fur of Fisher's head, wondering how he would ever be able to tell Petee what Max had done. He kept wiping away at the mud, feeling more and more heartsick. Finally, he just moved the tiny body over into the sink, and using the dish rinser, washed all the mud out of the cat's fur. Philip noticed then that Max hadn't torn the cat up any, no holes or rips. Philip smoothed out the fur with his hand, and slowly an idea developed in his head. He ran upstairs and got Marie's blow dryer and a comb.

As he blew the fur dry and combed it out, he thought, *Maybe if I could just sneak over there, and leave him on the porch, Petee can come out in the morning and find him, and he'll think Fisher just died in his sleep of natural causes.*

And that's just what Philip did. He got old Fisher all dried out and brushed clean. Then he chained up Max and sneaked across the street and up onto Petee's porch. He lay Fisher up on top of that window unit and kind of stretched him out there like he was dreaming about the bay. Then he snuck back home, swearing to himself that he would not tell even Marie his secret.

Next morning, Marie got up and got herself ready for the drive downtown while Philip fixed them both some pancakes. They ate while they read the paper, and Marie left for work while Philip cleaned up the dishes and had a second cup of coffee. When he went out to get in his car to go to work, he saw Petee Boudreaux standing out on the front porch with the couple from the house next door. Philip backed the car out of the driveway, thinking, *Now would be a good time to let myself in on the discovery. I'll stop the car and walk up the steps, and ask "What happened?"*

So he did. When he got to the top of the porch steps they were all standing around that window unit just staring. Poor Petee was shaking his head, when Philip said, "Oh, no! Ah, what happened?"

Petee just kept shaking his head, and Philip put his hand on Petee's shoulder and repeated his inquiry. "What happened?"

Petee looked at him, just realizing he was there, then shook his head again and said, "I don't know. It sure do beat de hell out of me, I guarantee. Ol' Fisher, he died on Friday and I buried him dere in de back yard. It is strange, fo' sure. Yep, it sure do beat de hell out of me."

Philip quietly backed down the steps, unnoticed by the little gathering on the porch. He got in his car and drove to work. On the way he got to thinking about the whole affair, and he reckoned that Petee hadn't quite got it right. Ol' Petee had called it "strange." But from where Philip was standing it wasn't so much strange as it was bizarre.

Yep, bizarre. That was the word for it. For you see, where Philip came from, it wasn't strange at all for a person to try his best to keep a friend from feeling hurt. He also knew that when you make your living making decisions before all the facts are in, sooner or later, you're going to guess wrong.

A Sprinkle Under the Summer Moon

JAY STAILEY

Although there is a shred of truth in every tale I tell, this one has more of the truth than most others. Moments after I told this story at the Saturday afternoon concert during the 1989 Texas Storytelling Festival, we all watched as the TWU automatic sprinkler system kicked on at the top of the hill next to the library. Slowly, more sprinklers began to spin, ever closer to the tent, while participants were assured that Maintenance had been notified of our presence and that there was nothing to be worried about. Seconds later, when the sprinkler heads inside the tent spun into action, some quick-thinking storytellers, armed with empty garbage cans, saved the festival from its first-ever indoor rainout.

There on the island, the best place to watch the sunset is over at Rolf Park. For us, the best time of year is in the summer months. From Rolf Park, or the hill park as my kids call it, you can look to the west over Clear Lake as the sun sinks slowly into the lakewaters. From atop the little hills, we watch as the shrimp boats, headed in to dock, and the sailboats, headed out to cruise, pass each other over the luscious orange streak that stretches from beyond the hotel on the north shore right up to the shoreline in front of us. On signal, as the sun dips into the water and disappears until dawn, the crickets and bullfrogs begin their nocturnal chorus and continue their serenade as we return home to our side of the island.

On one such July evening last summer, we set out to Rolf Park to witness that glorious sight, both the girls on their bikes and me with the dog in tow. I arrived to see the sun paint the wispy clouds yellow, then orange, then red and purple, and was serenaded by the happy shouts of the girls running up the little hills in the park and rolling down the other sides. The girls finally got quiet when the light disappeared, and on cue the crickets and frogs took up their joyful chatter. I sent the girls ahead on their bikes. I had decided the dog and I needed the exercise, so we took the long way home.

It had been a particularly dry month on the island, as it had been throughout the country. The bullfrog chorus seemed smaller than past years,

143

but it was trying its best. When we turned onto Hawthorne I saw ahead of us a figure straddling his bike. As I approached, I recognized Mayor Keebler.

He was standing ever so quietly, one ear cocked. When I came nearer he explained that he was listening for sprinklers. Seemed he had been all over the island that day charting water use. He noted in incredible detail the current water supply-and-demand situation and began to explain the possibility of the city going to a voluntary conservation program or even a rationing system. As he was carrying on about the options, the most incredible golden summer moon rose out of Galveston Bay and began to climb its way into the sky. I was taken immediately with the knowledge that it was this same summer moon that I had viewed nearly twenty years under much different circumstances, and the memory came rushing back.

It was the evening of July 20, 1969. I had been invited to a Moon Party at the home of Glen Booker. It was Glen's idea to gather friends and view the occasion of man's first steps on the lunar surface. All Ohio was drawn to the news, and people in Dublin were no exception. We were proud that Neil Armstrong, a native Ohioan, would be the first to walk on the moon; and as students about to take our own historic steps into the senior year of high school, we saw this event as an omen of a bright future ahead.

I was personally interested in this gathering because a certain Claudine Avery had also received an invitation. Claudine was a shy but beautiful blonde classmate whose daddy owned the Pontiac agency in town. Most importantly, it was rumored that she was madly in love with me.

The Bookers lived out in Indian Run Estates on a big chunk of land. When I arrived, I immediately noted the bright red Pontiac Firebird parked on the circle. Most of the guests were milling about, their interest shared between the news coverage (conversations with the readying crew) and the pool table. Glen and Jim Dellmar were busy setting up a camera and tripod. They had decided to catch this moment in history on black and white film, on the black and white feed from the moon, on Glen's color Zenith. Bob Pavlock, my silver-toothed buddy, was busy lining people up to take their quarters at eight ball.

I was busy discreetly following Miss Avery from room to room trying to impress her with witty and knowledgeable comments. Stunning phrases like, "Whew, he sure can break that rack!" and "Wow, that's a great picture for such a distance!" fell from my mouth and were lost in the clatter and contact of pool balls and the *"Shh! Shh!"* of the news hounds. If my comments were not lost on Claudine, then I assumed her shyness was keeping her from showing any interest in my clever patter.

At length we forgot about pool and all other games and watched as men set foot on the moon for the first time. Amid all the excitement, I noticed Claudine walk out the patio doors into the night. I quietly got up and followed. She was standing a few steps off the patio staring up at this big beautiful summer moon. I approached and stood beside her.

"It's incredible," she said.

"Yes, incredible," I agreed.

Long moments of silence. Our eyes gazed upward. Our knuckles bumped. Once. Twice. The third time we hung on for dear life.

"It's really incredible," I said.

"Yes, it really is," she agreed.

My gaze followed the Big Dipper down to the horizon and over to her silhouette. I waited for her to turn, but the wait became uncomfortable. As I turned my eyes back to the sky I could have sworn she looked my way. Did she? I cut my eyes back and … did she just look away? And again we looked but our gaze didn't meet. And a third and fourth time.

Finally we looked at the same time. I could see the stars in her eyes, and as I bent to kiss her I must have been blinded by the light. I missed to the lower left and planted one firmly on her chin. On any other night that could have spelled disaster. But tonight, we knew, was not just any night. Tonight, man was walking on the moon! And if that could happen, then anything could happen. We backed up and tried again. There under that canopy of stars and that great huge summer moon we kissed. *One small step for man*, I thought, *one giant leap for me!*

"It's incredible!" It was Mayor Keebler talking. The automatic sprinkling system had kicked on at the big house that looks out on the channel.

"That's the third time today," he said, as he pulled out a notebook and made a notation. Then he started in reporting whose houses had automatic systems and who watered by hand. Again the moon caught my eye. It was higher in the night sky now and didn't appear as large. The color had changed to silver-white, and once more my mind wandered off in the direction of the moon.

It was three years after Neil Armstrong's walk that I saw just such a summer moon at a wedding. I was still dating Claudine, and it was her brother Carl who was getting married. The father of the groom had rented a suite of rooms on the second floor of a hotel southeast of Cleveland, near the bride's home and the Catholic church where the wedding was to take place. Claudine and I arrived after the rehearsal dinner, just as the party at the hotel swung into action. Beginning to gather in one room were the bride and groom, friends of the two, and the numerous Avery cousins who were converging for the occasion from all over the northeastern United States. In the adjoining room were the adults: the parents of the bride and groom, business associates of both, and the multitude of Avery aunts and uncles who had delivered the aforementioned cousins.

I was, in Claudine's family, considered an honorary if not future member, and was not surprised as I stood near the door between the rooms to feel the hand of her father on my shoulder. His voice boomed, "Come on in, son, meet my friends and family."

Did he say "son"? I thought, feeling very satisfied. The smile on my face grew as he introduced me as a fine young man who would make any man proud to have as a son-in-law. I tried to look the part, shaking hands and smiling until he got sidetracked with the arrival of his brother Emil, in from Rhode Island. I found myself near the sliding glass door, bending down to talk to Claudine's mother.

"Yes, I am having a lovely time."

"Yes, it is great to meet more of the family."

"Yes, I will get another drink in a minute."

And, *Yes*, I thought, *it is getting awfully crowded, I think I will step out on the balcony for a moment.* In the glow of the revelry, I resisted the urge to tell her, "Mom, I'll be back in a minute." Instead I stepped silently out onto the balcony.

I slid the door closed and looked up. There it was! The big silver-white summer moon. Amid the mix of voices coming from the adults and the young people in the room off the next balcony, I stared up in awe. It seemed to be getting bigger as I watched. I squinted, believing that I could catch a glimpse of that little rigid American flag that Neil Armstrong had planted. As I squinted I was overcome by this frightening emptiness, and I felt a need to be with Claudine.

I turned, only to notice that the adult room was packed and that any attempt to venture into that sea of humanity would mean a discussion with Uncle Jack about the Cleveland Indians, or a long introduction to Uncle Emil or enormous Great-Aunt Emma, who had been directed by two of Emil's oldest sons into a chair in the middle of the room. It looked like a pretty permanent placement, a placement that blocked the line between me and my own true love.

As the noise from the next room floated out onto the adjacent balcony an idea struck me. I felt the wall separating my balcony from that of my beloved. It was no more than six inches thick. *Simple,* I thought. *I just stand on the balcony rail, hold onto the wall, swing one leg around, then the other, hop down and viola! She's at my side.* I beamed at the sheer genius of the idea.

With one last look at that moon, I embarked on my adventure. Up onto the balcony rail I leapt. Both hands on that wall, fingers firmly grasping the siding, I swung that first leg around. Then, as I straddled the wall, the siding came loose. I had seen this scene so many times as a child on "Abbott and Costello" and "The Three Stooges." Two-and-a-half stories up, as the siding pulled away from the hotel, I looked down at the sidewalk and the parking lot and cast my eyes up to the moon.

I had always heard under such circumstances one's life rushes before one's eyes. I should have known it would be different with me. As I began that long arching fall from the wall to the pavement below, I saw my future pass before me. It looked very bleak in terms of my standing with the Avery family. My stock was falling faster than I was, but I was picking up speed and would probably hit rock bottom at the same time it did. My brain was shouting *Sell! Sell!* the instant before my fingers let go and I plummeted to the earth.

I hit grass with the lower half of my body and was lucky that the hardest part of my anatomy hit the sidewalk. I rolled over and took only a glancing blow as the twenty-foot piece of siding arrived directly after me. Quickly I lifted the wood out of the sidewalk and parking lot and stashed it in a row of bushes. I ran to the steps and sat down to compose myself. Checking my body, I found only a torn shirt and bloody elbow. After a bit I went up to join the younger set but was no sooner in the door than the bride-to-be caught a glimpse of me and said, "What happened to you? You look like you've seen a ghost!"

As the phone rang in the next bedroom I thought, *Worse than a ghost, I've seen the future.*

Claudine's father picked up the phone. "The manager? The side of the hotel? Just a minute."

There was complete silence.

"Ten minutes," Mayor Keebler said. "The sprinkler ran for ten minutes."

He made a note in his book, and then it started up again. His eyebrows went up as the water reached its apex and went down just as suddenly as the sprinkler petered out and trickled to a stop. Then we heard the sprinkling sound again, but no water was coming out. Mayor Keebler just waited, watching the sprinkler heads, but I looked down and realized that my dog was the one sprinkling, and right on the mayor's shoes.

"Well, I got to go," I said, giving a jerk to the dog's leash. "Hope you get the water thing worked out after a while."

"Be careful," he shouted as I turned on to East Shore Drive. "Strange things can happen under a summer moon."

I turned back with the intention of shouting, "You don't know the half of it!" But I moved on without comment. He was looking down and shaking his foot. He'd soon enough find out the half he didn't know.

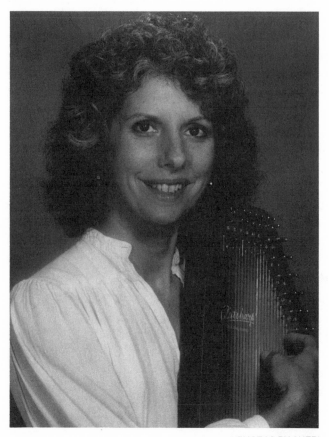

Traditionally trained in storytelling since childhood, FRAN STALLINGS has traveled the nation as a professional teller since 1978. She has worked extensively with thousands of K-12 students through State Arts Council of Oklahoma residencies. At festivals, she is known for tales with a sly twist or an intriguing touch of darkness. Her publications include fiction, professional articles, and original songs. She lives in Bartlesville, Oklahoma, where she directs the SunFest Storytelling Festival.

Shingebiss and the North Wind

FRAN STALLINGS

I grew up hearing this story as "a Chippewa legend." Trying to research its origins, I reached a dead end in the 1890s, when several children's versions first appeared. Ron Evans, an elder of the Chippewa Nation, thinks it's unlikely that the story is authentic Chippewa. My best guess, currently, is that it must be one of the "Indian style" stories composed for children by Caucasian-American authors of that period. Whatever the origins, it is a powerful story of learning to conquer fear. It is a favorite of both the women and the children at our local domestic violence shelter.

Long, long ago the People could not stay in their northern homes when winter came. They had to go south, like the birds, like the buffalo. Because of Old Man North Wind.

Old Man North Wind came down from northwest country. His head-dress was made not of feathers, but of icicles. His clothes were made of ice and snow. The features of his face were fierce, twisted with hate for all living things—plant, animal, and human.

When he blew his frosty breath—*phah!*—everything froze. The leaves on the trees died and fell to the ground. Fruits, nuts, seeds, all were destroyed. There was no more food. It was too cold to live. Those animals who could not sleep all winter in hollow places must go south. The People went, too.

But one year a young woman named Shingebiss rebelled. "It's not fair!" she said. "Why should we have to leave our homes, just because Old Man North Wind comes? I'm going to stay."

Some of the People told her, "No, Shingebiss, you cannot stay here. You will freeze. You will starve! Come south with us."

But Shingebiss refused. "I'm not afraid. Old Man North Wind is just a living creature, like us." And she sang:

North Wind, North Wind, fierce of feature,
You are still my fellow creature.

Blow your worst, you can't scare me.
I'm not afraid, and so I'm free.

Others of the People tried to change her mind, but Shingebiss would not come with them. So they said goodbye, certain that they would never see her alive again. And they went south.

Then Shingebiss began to work. She built a new kind of lodge, not thin-walled and breezy like the summer lodges of the People, but with thick double walls. She stuffed every crack with dry grass and moss, to keep out the wind. Then she collected great piles of dry wood and kept it handy by her door, so that she could keep her fire going at all times.

She was warm and comfortable. And she sang:

North Wind, North Wind, fierce of feature,
You are still my fellow creature.
Blow your worst, you can't scare me.
I'm not afraid, and so I'm free.

But then Old Man North Wind came down out of the far northwest. He blew his frosty breath—*phah!*—and everything died. But he saw the smoke rising from Shingebiss's fire. He saw her lodge.

"Who is this?" he asked. "Who is this, who dares to defy me?"

He blew his frosty breath at Shingebiss's lodge—*phah!*—but the wind could not get in. Shingebiss just piled more wood on the fire and sang:

North Wind, North Wind, fierce of feature,
You are still my fellow creature.
Blow your worst, you can't scare me.
I'm not afraid, and so I'm free.

"Hah!" said Old Man North Wind. "She cannot live without food." He blew his frosty breath on the lake—*phah!*—and it was covered with ice. "Now she can't catch fish," he said.

But Shingebiss just walked out onto the ice. She found tall reeds growing up through the ice. She pulled some of them out, leaving a hole! She caught fish *through* the ice. She carried them home, cooked them, ate them, and was warm and comfortable. And she sang:

North Wind, North Wind, fierce of feature,
You are still my fellow creature.
Blow your worst, you can't scare me.
I'm not afraid, and so I'm free.

Now Old Man North Wind was really angry. "I'll show her!" He blew his frosty breath and froze her ice-fishing holes. But she just walked out on the ice, pulled up more reeds, and made other holes to fish through.

"I must teach this Shingebiss a lesson," said Old Man North Wind. He followed her home to her lodge. He blew around and around it, but she just built up her fire and was warm and comfortable.

"So," said Old Man North Wind, "I will come inside." He stepped in the door.

Shingebiss was sitting by her fire. She added another log, and sang:

> North Wind, North Wind, fierce of feature,
> You are still my fellow creature.
> Blow your worst, you can't scare me.
> I'm not afraid, and so I'm free.

Old Man North Wind came closer to Shingebiss. He sat down right next to her! But she just stirred the fire and added more wood. The flames rose higher, and higher …

Old Man North Wind began to notice that his headdress of icicles was drooping … His clothes of ice and snow were becoming soggy, and full of holes … Drops of water began running down his face. "What is this? It can't be tears: *I* never cry! This can only mean that—I'm *melting!*"

Old Man North Wind ran out of Shingebiss's lodge and rolled in the snow until he was all frozen again. "That Shingebiss," he said. "She is too clever for me. I will leave her alone." And he did.

In the spring, when the other people returned, they were amazed to find Shingebiss alive and well. "We thought you would freeze and starve! We thought we would find nothing but your bones!"

Shingebiss said, "There are ways to keep warm and comfortable. There are ways to find food. I can teach them to you, so that we need not ever leave our homes again. But you can't stay if you are afraid."

So Shingebiss taught her People how to build winter lodges, how to collect fuel. She taught them to fish through the ice. And she taught them the song, so that they could sing together:

> North Wind, North Wind, fierce of feature,
> You are still my fellow creature.
> Blow your worst, you can't scare me.
> I'm not afraid, and so I'm free.

BRUCE DAVIS

FINLEY STEWART was nine years old when the first National Storytelling Festival took place back in 1972; in a real sense he's among the first generation of children who grew up during the storytelling renaissance in America. Since 1985, he has performed all over the United States from Point Barrow, Alaska, to Long Island, New York, and several stops in-between. The founder and current executive director of both the Texas Storytelling Festival and the Tejas Storytelling Association, he has twice been named to the position of chair of the National Storytelling Conference. He currently teaches a course in storytelling at the University of North Texas near his Denton home.

The Day Daddy Went to Church

FINLEY STEWART

Of all the stories that my mother shared with me growing up, this is probably the most memorable. For years, the telling of this story became a ritual during the Thanksgiving and Christmas holidays. As with all family stories, this tale has changed quite considerably for the telling.

Momma always went to church. Ever since I could remember, Momma had gone to Christ United Methodist Church in a small suburb of Dallas, Texas, called Farmers Branch. It sounded rural, but it wasn't—it was as big city as you could get in Dallas during the seventies.

You remember the seventies—shag carpet, mood rings, pet rocks, and fake wood paneling. Sure, everyone can reminisce about ice cream trucks charming the sidewalk, getting a soda at the drugstore, or even traveling door-to-door on Halloween, but those of us who came to be fully omniscient in the seventies remember the year all those things died. It was the seventies—bell bottoms and leisure suits, mellow yellow and "Puff the Magic Dragon." It was the seventies—when sex was safe and sky-diving was dangerous.

In those days there were five children—but only three of us "had to" go to church. Two had hit that age when they didn't "have to" go to church. But my brother Keith, and sister Janis and I *had to* go to church.

Momma always went to church. Every single Sunday she went to church. I was nine years old, and church seemed a very strange place to be. Each Sunday as we strolled in and "took our pew"—in the Methodist Church you don't just sit down; everything is a community event—it seemed as if the whole world was watching. It was Mother, then me, then Janis, and Keith.

Always after the sermon one of those good Christian women with blue hair who sat on the front row would stop Momma as we were leaving: "So—where's your husband?"

My mother's face would turn blood red and she would always make up some excuse for why Daddy couldn't come to church.

You see, that was the thing: Daddy *never* went to church. Oh, he was a good Methodist, all right, but he did not go to church. He went to Southern Methodist University, but he did not go to church.

One Sunday, Momma decided that she was gonna get Daddy to go to church. It was Christmas, and we had all just had a serious run-in with sister Thelma Parker, who was a charter member of the front-row society there at Christ United. Momma decided then and there that she was gonna get Daddy to go to church. She even set a date. By Easter, she was gonna get Daddy to go to church.

I remember when she asked him. I was sitting underneath the kitchen table. It was a large expansive thing that seemed like it sat thirty people at a time, but only sat six. But back then even a simple kitchen table had its own world about it.

I remember it well. She asked politely at first. "Allen," she said, "how would you like it if you went to church?"

There was a short pause. My father was probably in total disbelief that the question could have been asked. Then a short reply, *"No!"*

Momma followed, "Allen! *You're going to church!"*

Oh, the screaming and the fighting and the un-Christianlike words that were bantered back and forth. Never anything physical—always verbal. But Momma didn't stop there. She began to burn his dinner on purpose. She refused to wash his underwear. She began to eat and gnaw away at my father's very Scottish existence.

Now if my father had been any more Scottish, he would have been Presbyterian, not Methodist. And he was. Was. But remember, Mother was a Methodist, and this was Texas, and he did marry my mother. So.

Slowly it became clear to Daddy that his date with the Methodist church was inevitable. Finally, one day, Daddy decided he was going to church, but no sooner than Momma's deadline—on Easter.

We all got new clothes. Not because it was Easter, but because Daddy was going to church. My sister got a pink frill dress with black patent leather shoes and lace socks. It was funny, because she was fifteen at the time and was more into Janis Joplin than lace socks. She looked eight. I got new clothes, too—a leisure suit. A red denim leisure suit with a blue tie. I looked like a Republican. By this time my brother Keith had gotten to that age that he didn't *have to* go to church.

Mother held her head high as we entered the sanctuary. Her face showed her pride. Her makeup was impeccable. She even wore her best wig! She introduced Daddy to all the good blue-haired Christian women on the front row. "See, I really do have a husband!"

Then, we took our pew—first Daddy, then Momma, then me, and then Janis. The preacher started his sermon. Methodist preachers love the Ten

Commandments: Thou shall not do this. Thou shall not do that. If you ever do this one, we're gonna get you but good.

Looking back on it all, I guess it was too much for Daddy. Because that's when we heard it. It was kind of quiet at first. Could it be? No. Yes. A snore. A simple gasp of total relaxation.

My mother punched him in the side. "Allen," she whispered, "wake up."

He returned fairly quickly to consciousness. The preacher was warning us all of our sins. "I'm sorry, honey, I won't do it again."

The preacher continued his sermon. Sin and more sin, it almost sounded like a Baptist sermon. Louder this time we heard: *"Schhhgghhh."*

"Allen, wake up, you're embarrassing me." The good blue-haired Christian women on the front row started to turn their head and give momma The Eye. She punched him in the side. "Wake up right now!"

Daddy managed to rouse himself, "Oh I'm sorry, baby, I won't do it again. I'm sorry. I won't do it again."

As the preacher was getting around to the ninth of the ten, my father came to bat for the third time. Louder still. Resounding through the entire cathedral we heard him snore. It was long, and bumpy. Wheezing and gasping. Drawn out like a bad NBC mini-series. The type of body function that everyone tries to ignore and pretends never happened. The snore filled the church with more resonance than even the preacher could manage.

He stopped his sermon.

Everyone was looking at my momma. Her face was blood red. She did all she could do. She took her best elbow, and she punched him just as hard as she could punch him.

And he must have been dreaming, because when he woke, he stood up, puckered his lips, and shouted just as loud as he could shout. *"Hhhhhmmmm.* Kiss me, baby. Kiss me, quick!"

And that's the last time Daddy ever went to church.

Driving Down Memory Lane

FINLEY STEWART

It's sometimes funny where life takes you. My father was a geologist who traveled all around the United States looking for rocks. Now I'm a storyteller traveling all around the United States looking for stories. I guess that kind of stuff is just passed on through the genes. In my childhood, my dad showed me almost every state in the Union—by car. This travel story, which is mostly true, always brings back fond memories for me.

Every summer my family drove to Pennsylvania. We had the money to fly, but my father always insisted on driving. He was born and reared in Pennsylvania. Every summer Daddy loaded us in the car and pointed it toward home.

Home for him was a little community called Tower Hill 2, outside of Merritstown, outside of Republic, outside of Uniontown, outside of a little town called Pittsburgh. Home for him was Aunt Jeannie, his sister, who still lived in their old family homestead. The house was over a hundred years old. That's old to a small boy from Texas, where anything over twenty-five is labeled an antique. Home for him was the winding mountain roads, the smell of lignite, the taste of wild blackberries growing along the side of the road. Home for him really was a place where you walked to school through six feet of snow, barefoot, uphill, both ways.

It was coal country. Or at least it had been at some point. By my childhood the coal mines had been closed. The mines were only a few hundred yards from my daddy's homestead. And although I never saw them in action, I could well imagine them in their boom. Each summer my father would take me down the winding path to the ruins of the coal mines: old red-brick buildings with roofs that must have caved in long ago; ivy growing on the side of buildings with portions of walls missing; old coal and lignite mounds all but covered with layers of vines of blackberries and weeds and trees. Each year, we would walk those mines and Daddy would show me where my grandfather, for whom I was named, worked as a blacksmith.

"Step here," Dad would say. "No ... not there ... here." And we would retrace steps my father had walked long ago, careful to not step on the wrong mound of vegetation, or the ground beneath our feet would give way to the coal mines beneath the surface. He told me stories of the mine in its heyday, of bringing Momma to meet his mother for the first time.

Mother told me stories too. Of how one year the snow piled so high that the only way they could get in and out of my father's house was to walk out a second-story window. Of how, wanting to impress his family, she—a Texas native—washed all the clothes and hung them out to dry. You don't hang clothes out to dry in coal country. In minutes they were all blackened with soot. Of how they had to walk to an outhouse just to use the bathroom—an outhouse that even in my youth still stood. Daddy was on his way home.

Every year we drove to Pennsylvania at breakneck speeds. We always drove straight through, twenty-four hours straight through. On the rare occasion that the car forced Daddy to refuel, we would all clamor to get in line. The first line was the bathroom. The second line was for the drink machine, ten cents for an Orange Crush or a chocolate soda. My dad always made me save the bottle.

We had an old 1967 Cougar. It was sporty in those days. Red. There was a whole world in the floorboard of that car. It seemed that the car housed circuses, battlegrounds, even alien planets! A few hours after the pit stop, though, it was clear that the car needed one more thing—a bathroom. Daddy would never stop. I came to know the humiliation of what every boy has to endure on long car trips. I came to know why my dad always made me save the bottle; even my sister was forced to use it, an engineering feat that I still to this day can't comprehend—and don't ask about.

One year on our way to Pennsylvania, my dad decided to take a small detour to visit some relatives in California. On our way to California, we stopped for a rare refueling in Santa Fe, New Mexico. We all piled out of the car to take our customary stand in line for the bathroom, followed by visits to the drink machine for an Orange Crush or even a chocolate soda.

As we turned back to pile in the car, my dad was standing at the door. The driver's side door was wide open; his arm rested on the top of the door. There was a big smile on his face. He said, "You know, the last time I was in Santa Fe, New Mexico, over by the railroad station, sitting on a stump by the railroad tracks, there was this old, old Indian with deep-set eyes that look right through you. Cracks and lines in his face as deep as canyons, and long gray hair. And do you know that he had such a good memory that he could tell you what he did on any day of his life?"

We all said sure, Dad, sure. And we piled into the car to finish our detour. "No," he said, "I'm serious." And then, as if somehow trying to prove his manhood, he drove us to the railroad station. And there, sure enough, sitting on a stump by the railroad tracks was that old, old Indian.

Believe it or not, he was still there. My father was indeed right. The battle of time had just helped reinforce the image my father had created. He did have deep-set eyes that looked right through you, cracks and lines in his face as deep as canyons, and long gray hair.

"He can tell you what he did on any day of his life," my father said. "There—one of you go up there and ask him. He'll prove it."

I was the youngest. I was about ten at the time. I was defenseless. I was chosen. "Finley, go ask him what he did on any day of his life—he can remember, he'll tell you!"

I had never met an Indian before. I had only seen them blown away in old John Wayne films. Even the thought scared me. My father pushed me along as he so often did. "Ask him. He can tell you what he did on any day of his life."

I walked up to him. I said, "Hello, Mr. Indian. My father tells me that you can tell me what you did on any day of your life. And if that's true, I was wondering, could you please tell me what you had for breakfast on March 5, 1942."

That old, old Indian with deep-set eyes that looked right through you, cracks and lines in his face as deep as canyons, and long gray hair, just looked at me and said, "Eggs."

I walked back to my father. He was shaking his head in disappointment. After all, anyone could have said that he had eggs for breakfast. But we had to get back on the road. We had to get to Pennsylvania by way of California. So we all climbed back in and went to California, and on to Pennsylvania, and had a wonderful summer.

And if it were not for fate and life and storytelling, this story would have ended there. But it didn't. Years later, many years later, my old storytelling partner, James Howard, and I were telling stories in tandem, billing ourselves as the StoryWeavers. In the beginning finances were short: we did far more telling than billing.

One year, maybe in 1986, we were invited to New Mexico to tell stories. It seemed it would be a prestige gig. Not only would we get paid a thousand dollars for two days' work (that's a lot of money to a twenty-one year old college student), we would also get the opportunity to tell stories to ninety thousand people at one of the largest events in the world! What a grand opportunity! Ninety thousand people. And believe it or not, it did happen. We stood before ninety thousand people and told stories. The problem was that no one listened. Balloons were being launched. The Blue Angels were flying test patterns overhead. People were eating, people were talking, people were sleeping, everything, anything but listening to stories.

On the way back from this dismal experience to the airport, the woman who had invited us suggested that we drive the few extra miles to see Santa

Fe. "You'll love it!" she said. "All that adobe, and the fake adobe, and the fake, fake adobe."

Once we reached Santa Fe, she stopped her van at a small gas station to get gas. Everyone piled out of the van for bathrooms and such. When they returned, I was standing at the driver's door of the van. It was wide open. My arm was placed as close to the top of the door as it could get. I had a big smile on my face. I said, "You know, the last time I was in Santa Fe, New Mexico, over by the railroad station, sitting on a stump by the railroad tracks there was this old, old Indian with deep-set eyes that could look right through you; cracks and lines in his face as deep as canyons, and long gray hair. And do you know that he had such a good memory that he could tell you what he did on any day of his life?"

Jim said, "Yeah, yeah, right, put it in a book, let's get out of here, we have more fake adobe to see."

I said, "No, it's true. I'll take you there." I grabbed the keys from the woman's hand and shoved her to the side. I took control of the wheel, everyone piled in, and I drove us to the railroad depot. And there, sure enough, sitting on a stump by the railroad tracks, was that old, old Indian. Believe it or not, he was still there. He had deep-set eyes that looked right through you. Cracks and lines in his face as deep as canyons, and long gray hair.

"He can tell you what he did on any day of his life," I said. "There—one of you go up there and ask him. He'll prove it."

Obviously, no one would.

"I'll prove it to you," I said.

I marched up to that old Indian and began my query. Now remember, the only Indian other than him that I had ever seen was in John Wayne films. This was at least a year before I discovered something close to a real Native American. I held to the cinematic myth of the Native American culture. I tried my best to be Indianlike. I marched up to him and, in my best Indian voice, said, "How."

And that old, old Indian, with deep-set eyes that looked right through you, just looked at me and said: "Scrambled."

Now, it's important to note that most of this story is true. There really is an Indian in Santa Fe. I really am a storyteller. And my dad really did walk to school through six feet of snow, barefoot, uphill, both ways.

Lady Ragnell

FINLEY STEWART

A friend of mine calls this old tale the story of 1992—she claims that in that year every storyteller in the nation was telling it—and she may be right. This old legend has had many settings and many tellers, among the recent ones Gioia Timpanelli and Heather Forest. Chaucer told this story, Shakespeare told this story. I've been telling this story since 1987, and along the way I have encountered more than forty different versions of the tale—here's mine.

King Arthur was walking through the woods one day with a satchel of arrows upon his back, when soon he came upon a wood he had not seen before. He was just about to leave when he heard a thunder upon thunder, a roar upon roar, and a crash upon crash: there before him, some ten feet tall, with his great black armor, helmet, and sword, stood a great black knight.

The knight looked down upon Arthur and spoke, "You have been hunting in my wood, and for that you must die!"

The knight took his mighty sword, grabbed Arthur by the neck, and was about to take his head, when Arthur spoke, "I am Arthur, King of Camerlon. There must be some mistake, for I knew not that it was your wood!"

"Well," the knight replied, "perhaps some deal we can here make. Let us play a little game to see which of us is just! We'll take turns chopping off each other's heads!" And the knight threw his sword to Arthur.

Arthur looked at the great black sword; he held it in his hand. *What a gruesome game,* he thought, *but surely the knight has given me the first chance. I'll but chop off his head and return to the castle.*

The great knight lowered his head down upon a nearby stump. Arthur lifted the great black sword and ... *THUMP! Cachink, cachink, cachink.* The great knight's head rolled and hit a nearby tree.

Arthur put down the sword and was about to walk away when suddenly the great knight lifted up his body, walked over to the tree, picked up his head, placed it back upon his shoulders and said "My turn!"

160

The great black knight grabbed his sword and took Arthur by the neck. Arthur looked up upon his challenger and said, "Could there not be some other deal that we might make? For I know if you chop off my head, it will not go back on."

Surely the great knight must have felt pity for Arthur that day, for he looked at him and said, "All right, old boy, we'll play ourselves a little riddle. If you can answer me this riddle within one year's time, then you shall keep your head. But if you cannot answer me this riddle within one year's time, then your head will be mine, Arthur of Camerlon. Meet me back here in this wood, within one year's time, with the answer to this: name it, what is it, the one thing that a woman wants most?"

Arthur smiled, for he thought he knew that answer. Most men do: *think* they know the answer. "All right," he said, "this game we shall play." And he watched as the great knight mounted his stallion and disappeared through the trees.

Arthur walked all the way back to Camerlon, wondering what it was, the one thing that a woman wants most. As he made his way down the path, he met some women, and as he met them, he began to ask what it was, the one thing that a woman wants most. Some said love. Some said money. Some said children—lots and lots of children. Still others said—sleep!

He asked every single woman he met what it was, the one thing that a woman wants most, and every single one of them had a different answer. He even asked his own wife Guinevere, but her answer seemed no better than the rest. No one answer stood out from the rest. He spent an entire year's time asking every single woman he met what it was, the one thing that a woman wants most.

A year passed, and on the very day he was to meet the great knight, Arthur was walking down a path, where there by a stream, sitting on a log was … a woman? *It must be a woman,* he thought, but he couldn't be sure: for he looked at her, and she had a roll of fat, over a roll of fat, over a roll of fat. She had long gray hair that grew from her head—and from her legs! She had one long lip that reached down to her first layer of fat. Arthur thought to back away, when she turned and she spoke to him, and she said, "Arthur! Don't go away. I know what it is that you want. You want to know what it is, the one thing a woman wants most—and Arthur, only I have the answer! If you will do me my bidding, I will tell you the answer to the secret you seek."

Arthur could not believe his eyes. The woman was so ugly he could not witness it all with just one glance: she had scabs and sores all about her body. She was so grotesque that her knees were knobby, and pus ran from them. She was so ugly that her feet were small, and her bottoms—plural—were large.

"Good woman!" he spoke. "What is your name, and what is it that you seek?"

"My name … is Lady Ragnell. All that I ask in return is that you give me the hand of your most handsome knight, Sir Gawain, in marriage."

"I am sorry, milady, but this I cannot do. Sir Gawain is his own man, he has his own sovereignty, and I can promise his hand to no woman."

The woman cocked her head with a knowing glance. "I understand," she said, "but at least ask him. Ask him if he will but marry me, and then I'll tell you. I'll tell you what it is, the one thing a woman wants most!"

Arthur looked at the woman. She was so deformed that she had a hump upon her shoulder. So stricken from disease that her hands were not hands but more like claws. So malformed, that her teeth were not teeth but more like tusks. So downright ugly that she had one great eye in the center of her forehead and another … someplace else!

Today is the day, Arthur thought. "All right, old woman, we'll give it a try!"

Arthur made his way back to Camerlon, back to Sir Gawain. When Arthur set his eyes upon Sir Gawain, he could think only of his beauty. Sir Gawain was so handsome that his hair was of ebony black. Sir Gawain was so good-looking that his skin was of a deep dark brown. Sir Gawain was so handsome that all the women peered upon him—both day and night. Arthur told Gawain the whole story of meeting the old woman in the wood, and that if he would but marry her, then Arthur's own life might be saved.

And Sir Gawain, who was truly a most honorable knight said, "Sire, you are my king, and whatever you would ask, surely, I would do!"

"Hold on, old boy," said Arthur, "you haven't seen the old hag yet."

Arthur led Gawain down the path to where, near a stream, sitting upon a log was … Lady Ragnell. Sir Gawain looked at Lady Ragnell: the scabs and sores, knobby knees and pus, the bottoms, the humps, the claws, the tusks— the great eye! Worse yet, her nose was not a nose, but more like a snout—and there was something hanging from it.

Gawain turned to Arthur and spoke, "Arthur, you are my king, and I shall marry this woman!"

Lady Ragnell pulled Arthur's ear over, and she whispered in his ear the secret: what it is, the one thing that a woman wants most. Arthur wiped the mucus from his ear, and then he set out to that secret wood; for by now, it was time to meet the great black knight.

Once there, he heard a thunder upon thunder, a roar upon roar, and crash upon crash! Once again, standing before him, some ten feet tall, with great black armor, helmet, and sword was the great black knight. "If you wish to keep that head upon your shoulders, speak now, boy—speak! Name it, what is it, the one thing that a woman wants most?"

Arthur did not want to risk Sir Gawain's life so quickly to the old hag, so he offered other answers:

"Could it be a husband?"

The great knight sighed!

"Children?" said Arthur.

The knight's sigh turned to laughter.

"Equal pay for equal work?"

The great knight would take no more. He took his sword, he grabbed Arthur by the neck, and he was about to chop off the king's head when Arthur turned and said: "Could it be, the one thing that a woman wants most ... could it be ... her own sovereignty—the right to choose, her own free will?"

"Curses!" the knight shouted. "Only my sister could have told you!" The great knight mounted his stallion and disappeared through the trees. Arthur walked back down the path toward Camerlon, now knowing what it was, the one thing that a woman wanted most—her own sovereignty, her own free will. As he neared the castle Camelot, he saw throngs of people heading toward the castle. *Why would all these people be heading toward the castle?* he thought. The wedding! For surely now there must be a wedding, a wedding between Sir Gawain and Lady Ragnell!

As he entered, he saw that the great hall was full and festive. There was meat, there was fruit, there was drink. But no one ate, no one save Lady Ragnell. For she would pull open her lip down to the first layer of fat, pick up a side of beef, stick it in, and pull it out all bones again!

The time for the great wedding came. There were scores of people on both sides of the hall. As Sir Gawain and Lady Ragnell made their way down the aisle, the women, they cried. Some of the *men* cried. But soon they said their vows and they were married!

Sir Gawain took Lady Ragnell's hand and whisked her high up the stairs to the castle tower, to the bed chamber, where Lady Ragnell sat upon the bed. She looked at him with her one good eye and said, "Sir Gawain, could you do me one last request?"

"You are my wife," he said, "and surely whatever you would ask, I would do." Sir Gawain was truly a most honorable knight.

"Could you, but just, give me ... a kiss?"

She was his wife, and he was an honorable knight. He walked on over, bent down, and gave Lady Ragnell, just ... a kiss.

A kiss! he thought to himself as he covered his face from the sight of hers. But when he brought his hands down again, there standing before him was not that old hag but a beautiful, golden-haired woman!

"Are you ...?" he asked.

"Yes!" she answered. "I am Lady Ragnell. My wicked brother placed a curse upon me for some menial task that I refused to perform. But now,

163

Gawain, now that curse is broken. And now, Gawain, we shall be together. And now, Gawain, you have a choice. For you may choose me to be a beautiful woman by day and an old hag by night. Or an old hag by day and a beautiful woman by night! The choice is yours, Sir Gawain, and only you shall make it."

Sir Gawain thought for a very long time. But soon a smile rose to his face, and his hands rose with it. "I have it, milady! This choice, this choice that you so boldly speak of! It is not mine to make—but yours!"

She threw her arms around him and said, "Oh Gawain, you've done it! You've broken the curse altogether. And now I shall be beautiful by both day and night. For now I have what no man can give me—my own sovereignty, my own free will!"

The next morning, when Arthur and Guinevere knocked upon the chamber door, they saw Sir Gawain and this ... *woman!* Arthur wondered if Gawain had already gone mad and ditched the old hag. But then he looked into the woman's eyes and saw that it was Lady Ragnell, and he realized what must have happened. For that, Arthur threw them a great party, the likes of which few have ever seen. And from then on in the land of Camerlon, they lived happily ever after.

SYLVIA PITCHFORD

THE STORYWEAVERS are James Howard and Finley Stewart. They began telling in tandem while in college in 1985, and for four short years toured extensively throughout the Southwest telling participation tales to anyone who would listen. They were among the first tellers to be selected to perform at the Exchange Place at the National Storytelling Festival and, according to the *Dallas Times Herald,* quickly built a pre-pubescent following, "attracting children in numbers worthy of a Bruce Springsteen concert." Finley Stewart continues to tour nationally telling stories. James Howard chose to get a "real job" and currently teaches at a college near his home in Mesa, Arizona.

The Star Stealer

THE STORYWEAVERS

This old Texas legend was such a favorite of our audiences that it became our signature story. Telling the tale in tandem, we traded off lines, creating rhythm and participation. This was an instant hit with children, who freely participated in the tale—chanting "a vavoom, a vavoom, a vavoom!" We never had to ask them to join in, they simply picked up the rhythm, knowing when to vavoom *and when not to* vavoom. *To this day, people still ask for written versions of the story, of which we know none—until now.*

Out in West Texas it's flat. Flat as a tabletop it is. Every once in a while, though, you can see some mountains rising up out of the ground, but on top, they're flat. Flat as a tabletop. Out in West Texas they call them *mesas.* Now a long time ago, there was one mountain that was so high that it almost touched the sky. But on top it was flat: flat as a tabletop.

There used to live a village of people on that mountain: but it was so high they couldn't go down the mountain just any day they wanted. It was too high up; so they chose one day a year. And on that day, the people who lived on the mountaintop would climb down the mountain and visit the people who lived in the flatlands. They'd eat, dance, visit with each other, and have a big party.

One year, all the villagers who lived on the mountain made their way down to the flatlands, but the last to leave was a small boy. He looked back toward the mountaintop, and there he saw the oldest man of the village had remained behind. "Aren't you coming down to the party with us?" the little boy asked.

"Oh no, no. I'm getting too old for that kind of thing," said the old man. "I'll just stay up here and keep myself occupied. But you go on down and enjoy yourself!"

"Well, all right," said the boy, "but you're going to be all alone!" And the boy waved goodbye to the old man.

Now the old man, he was left all alone on that mountain that was flat as a tabletop. At first he thought it would be nice to have the whole mountain to himself, but he soon found out that there wasn't much to do. He got out his old garden hoe and tried gardening for a while, but soon night overtook him: he became weary and sat down on a rock for comfort. When he sat down, he looked up in the sky, and there he saw all the stars of the heavens—just glittering and twinkling. The old man thought to himself: *I sure would like to have one of those stars!* That mountain was so high, it almost seemed as if he could reach them. Without even thinking about it much, he stood up on that rock and lifted his garden hoe, as high as he could, into the heavens.

To his amazement, that old garden hoe actually caught the corner of one of those stars and it came falling down toward him. The star landed at the foot of the rock. It was bright and beautiful—like nothing he had seen before. The old man looked at the star on the ground for the longest time; then he realized that he both saw and heard the star. For it was making the most beautiful noise. The star at his feet was going, "A vavoom, a vavoom, a vavoom!"

The old man couldn't believe his ears! There was the star and it was going, "A vavoom, a vavoom, a vavoom." He reached down and picked up the star in his hand, and the star kept singing, "A vavoom, a vavoom, a vavoom." The old man loved the star so much, he thought he'd get another star.

So once again he stood on the rock and lifted his garden hoe as high as it could reach. He caught another star, and it too came crashing down, and it was going, "A vavoom, a vavoom, a vavoom." The old man picked up the first star and the second star, he held them close to his ears, and they were going, "A vavoom, a vavoom, a vavoom."

The old man got carried away, he stood on the rock and with his garden hoe took down another star, and another, and another. Soon there were no stars left in the sky: they were all down at his feet, and they were going, "A vavoom, a vavoom, a vavoom."

The old man stood upon the rock and conducted the stars as a heavenly orchestra, with his arms flaring and the mountainside glaring, as the stars were going, "A vavoom, a vavoom, a vavoom."

At some point the old man glanced down from the mountain and saw that all the villagers were finished with their party and making their way back up the mountainside. The old man knew he wasn't supposed to be stealing the stars. He knew he had to do something with them, so the opened up the door to his cabin and began to scoop up all the stars. He placed them all in his cabin and shut the door behind him. Now his cabin was going, "A vavoom, a vavoom, a vavoom." The old man stood inside the cabin and held back the stars from the door; their noise vibrated the logs of the cabin and he fell asleep.

Soon all the villagers returned to that mountain that was flat as a tabletop. They all noticed something was wrong. "Where are the stars?" they asked.

"Let's ask the old man," said another. "He was here—he should be able to tell us."

So they all gathered around the hut. They woke the old man. "Where are the stars?" they asked. "Where are all the stars?"

The old man rubbed his eyes. He knew that it was only a matter of time before the villagers found them, so he confessed the truth. "Well, you wouldn't believe me if I told you, but I had my old garden hoe, and I reached toward the sky and pulled down one of the stars. It was making the most beautiful noise—oh I wish you could have heard it! So I got another, and another … I'm afraid I stole all the stars from the sky!"

"You did *what?*" the villagers asked. "Well, you better put them back up there tonight!"

The old man opened the door to the cabin, and the villagers saw and heard the stars for themselves: they were packed so tightly in the cabin, they began to pull them all out, the stars all the while going, "A vavoom, a vavoom, a vavoom."

All the villagers took stars and placed them in their hands. They were going, "A vavoom, a vavoom, a vavoom." They tried to place the stars back in the sky, but they just fell back to the mountain going "A vavoom, a vavoom, a vavoom."

Someone said, "Let's try some glue."

So they took glue and spread it all over the stars and now the stars were going, "A vlavloom, a vlavloom, a vlavloom"—for that is what gluey stars sound like! They all reached their gluey stars toward the heavens, yet they fell back to earth going, "A vlavloom, a vlavloom, a vlavloom."

Now the little boy, the one who had first spoken with the old man, he loved those stars so much that he just took a star, wiped off all the glue, he made a wish and gave it a kiss and …

Vvvvvhhhhsssssmmm. The star flew back into the sky!

The old man saw that and he too picked up a star, wiped off the glue, made a wish and gave it a kiss and …

Vvvvvhhhhsssssmmm. It too flew back into the sky.

One by one, all the villagers did the same, and just as morning came, all the stars had been returned to the sky. They were glittering and twinkling, going, "A vavoom, a vavoom, a vavoom."

The villagers decided they had to do something with the old man; after all, he had been stealing the stars. Some of them wanted to kick him right off the mountaintop. But the little boy said, "No. No. The old man loved the stars just as much as we did, he just got a little greedy, that's all. What we ought to do is make him come out every night and count every single star to make sure that they're all there."

Everyone thought that was a good idea. So that night the old man went out counting: "A one, and a two …" Soon his friends joined him, then the neighbors. Soon even the children came out, but by then no was counting them, they were all lending an ear to the heavens, just listening to the stars going, "A vavoom, a vavoom, a vavoom."

To this very day, people out in West Texas are still sitting on their porches, just as evening breaks, counting the stars and listening to them: "A vavoom, a vavoom, a vavoom …"

Afterword

If you want to learn more about the storytelling movement and storytelling in general, contact us at the Tejas Storytelling Association. Through mailings, newsletters, telephone information lines, and events, TSA continues its mission to keep storytelling at the forefront of modern society.

We also encourage you to join us each March for the Texas Storytelling Festival. While reading these fine stories is indeed a treat, hearing them and those like them is even better—there is no substitution for the well-told tale. Each October, thousands also gather for the National Storytelling Festival in Jonesborough, Tennessee. In fact, throughout the year, there's probably some major storytelling event happening near where you live. To find out more information about these events and the organizations that sponsor them, contact TSA: we'll be glad to pass the word on.

Our storytellers always love feedback, so please feel free to write them in care of the address below.

The Tejas Storytelling Association
P.O. Box 2806
Denton, Texas 76202
817-387-8336

Permissions

"Mr. Cramer: A True Ghost Story of Houston" printed by permission of Jeannine Pasini Beekman. From the audiocassette *One Texan's Tales,* Spellweaver Productions, 10606 Clematis Lane, Houston, TX 77035. © 1989 Jeannine Pasini Beekman.

"La Cucarachita" and "Tío Conejo and the Hurricane" printed by permission of Mary Ann Brewer. "La Cucarachita" appears on two sound recordings available from Mary Ann Brewer: *Stories with Spunk and Spice* (told bilingually), © 1991 Mary Ann Brewer; and *"La Cucarachita" y Otros Cuentos Alegres ("La Cucarachita" and Other Lively Tales),* told completely in both English and Spanish, © 1995 Mary Ann Brewer.

"Maid Maleen" printed by permission of Nancy Burks.

"Speculation" and "A Man to Bank On" printed by permission of Charlotte Pugh Byrn. Both are from the audiocassette *Living Link,* Charlotte Byrn, 10315 Catlett Lane, La Porte, TX 77571. © 1993 Charlotte Pugh Byrn.

"The Story of Mahsuri," "Dad Watches the Moonwalk," and "The Legend of the Rainbow" printed by permission of Ted Colson.

"The Cook of El Rancho Cultural" printed by permission of Allen Damron. From the audiocassette *Storytelling 1—El Rancho Cultural,* Quahidi Records, Inc., 5107 Fort Clark, Austin, TX 78745. © Quahidi Records, Inc.

"The Birth of Oisin" printed by permission of Elizabeth Ellis.

"Miss Fanny Rollins of Pear Orchard, U.S.A." and "David and Goliath" reprinted by permission of Elizabeth Faulk. From the book *The Uncensored John Henry Faulk,* published by Texas Monthly Press. © Elizabeth Faulk.

"Johnson and the Red Bandanna" printed by permission of James Ford. From the audiocassette *Still Just Having Fun,* James Ford, 11811 I-10 East, Suite 185A, Houston, TX 77029. © 1992 James H. Ford.

"Pretzel-Faced Willie" printed by permission of Zinita Parsons Fowler.

"Another Bowl of Beans" printed by permission of Rodger Harris.

"Chocolate" and "With the Help of Sterling" printed by permission of Rosanna Taylor Herndon. "Chocolate" is from the audiocassette *A Boy Called "Chocolate" and Other Favorite Stories,* © 1994 Rosanna T. Herndon. "With the Help of Sterling" is from the audiocassette *The Sound of Clocks: Four Stories from Rosanna Herndon.* Both are available from Dr. Rosanna T. Herndon, 90 Bay Shore Ct., Abilene, TX 79602.

"An Old Nigerian Tale" printed by permission of Ayubu Kamau.

"Aunt Tucky" printed by permission of Harriet Lewis.

"Pandora" printed by permission of Barbara McBride-Smith. From the audiocassette *Greek or Whut?,* Pandora Productions, Route 2, Box 132, Stillwater, OK 74075. © 1989 Pandora Productions.